TRUE SACRIFICE

The Lost and Found Series
Book Two

Amanda Mackey

TRUE SACRIFICE

Limitless Publishing, LLC
Kailua, HI 96734
www.limitlesspublishing.com

Formatting: Limitless Publishing

ISBN-13: 978-1-64034-276-7
ISBN-10: 1-64034-276-1

Chapter One

Harley

The guy standing in front of me grinned and held out a meaty hand to shake. Upon seeing his face, memories of my dream shot like liquid fire through my brain, triggering a fight or flight response. My body tensed as I processed the haphazard snapshots. Fighting. Brothers. Comradery. Loyalty. Fierce protection. Unspoken words. Instinct. An unbreakable bond, threatened by war. It all came hard and fast, slamming into me, forcing me to stagger back. I continued to watch him. He continued to smile, his hand unwavering, waiting for me to reciprocate.

Clarity cut through the hazy muck as the first emotion since waking in the hospital bloomed in my chest. This guy meant everything to me. He'd had my back without question, and vice-versa. Till the death. Details eluded me, but knowin' he'd die for me had already been written in stone long ago and stamped into my psyche.

Regaining my composure and standing taller, a small smirk played at the edges of my mouth, which until now resembled a sharp slice of anxiety.

Sentiment swelled, the tide of my blood carrying it through my body. It seeped into the black crevices formed by amnesia.

Letting the smile engulf my face and surging forward, I embraced my best friend in a powerful hug, clapping him on the back, overcome with too much sensation. Tears beckoned, but I held them at bay as I swallowed hard and winced. My gunshot wound protested the gesture but I ignored it, not giving a shit about physical pain because to finally feel the connection of someone other than Mac had me all kinds of happy. A person from my past overrode any and all physical aches.

"Viper." Nothing else came out. We pulled back and scrutinized each other. His blond, buzzed hair sprouted from his scalp like new grass. Clean shaven face. Green eyes held mischief complementing the dimple on his left cheek.

"What's this bullshit about you not remembering me?" he balked, cutting to the chase.

I moved away, motioning for him to enter, swinging my arm wide. His eyes fell on Mac and then returned to me. An eyebrow rose in question.

Shutting the door, I found Mac intensely focused on both of us, her face lit with joy at our exchange. She too felt the connection from my past come to life.

She stood before I could answer my friend and came to greet him. "Hi. I'm Mac. We spoke on the phone."

Viper's eyes mapped her out. Assessing. Ogling. It took a moment for him to respond as he held out his hand. "My name's Charlie O'Dowell, but you can call me Viper."

She nodded, taking his hand for a brief shake and pointing to the sofa. "Nice to meet you, Viper. Please sit."

We took our places, me beside Mac in some territorial display of ownership. Viper sat on the single recliner beside us.

"So are you gonna answer me, douche?" Viper laughed, continuing his banter.

It wasn't offensive. In fact, it settled me. Much like Mac's presence. My subconscious knew. I needed it. Needed *normal*. The people surrounding me seemed like the only normal I had.

"I don't remember much at all. Seeing you though, it triggered the memory I had of us in Afghanistan. The day Reno…"

I stopped short upon seeing Viper's face scrunch and his eyes briefly flit to Mac before he cracked his neck and focused on me again.

"Sorry, man. I shouldn't have brought him up," I offered, realizing he may still be grieving.

"Don't worry about it. We both lost a friend that day." He shifted uncomfortably.

Mac rose to offer drinks. "Wine, Viper? Harley and I were having a couple before you arrived."

His face twitched as he acknowledged Mac. "Wine sounds good. I'd prefer beer, but I'll take what I can get." Turning back to me, he chuckled. "Harley, huh? That will take a bit of getting used to. Are you going to have everyone call you that?"

"Yep. It's who I am now. I associate myself with him."

"Fair enough. I'll call you whatever you want, including shit for brains. I'm just glad you're alive."

I laughed before adding, "You and me both, although waking up with no past leaves a lot to be desired."

"Any idea who shot you?" Viper asked, taking the glass from Mac as she sat down and handed me my refill.

"Terrorist. I'm certain. A snippet of that night came to me. I chased a lead on a planted explosive in a nightclub in town. Everyone evacuated. I searched in an alley. It's where the police found me. There's nothing after that."

"Hmm. It's possibly connected to the cell who captured and killed Reno. We killed their leader. Could be personal now. Any idea who asked you to investigate the bomb? I'd have known about it if it came from our unit."

Forcing out air, I sensed Mac's fear beside me. Her quiet curse and nervous shifting gave her away. Without looking, I squeezed her leg. It comforted me as well.

The thought of having a target on my back didn't sit well, and I sure as hell didn't want her involved.

"I got nothing else. Not sure where the order came from. So you don't know anything about it? That's odd."

"We get jobs on the sly sometimes. It's not unusual, although there's normally backup. You obviously had none and were flying solo." His pensive gaze across the room upped my pulse.

4

Being given a solo job, even without my memory, caused a flicker of unease to creep up my spine. It didn't sound like a typical job, but then what did I know?

More than ever, I needed to keep Mac safe if those who tried to kill me still wanted me dead.

We'd discussed me moving in with my ex-wife Trudy, who lived in a secure estate to offer some protection. Mac had insisted, even though I knew her heart said otherwise. Now, it seemed like I didn't have a choice. I needed to remove myself from her life to keep her safe.

Spinning around, I caught the worry swimming in her eyes, but I needed to stay strong. "I'm gonna move in with Trudy as planned. I don't want you involved in any of this shit. I mean it, Mac. I'll do whatever it takes to protect you."

Her frown deepened as her head fell downward, eyes focused on her lap.

"Ah, man you may want to consider moving in with me instead." Viper's husky, concerned drawl pulled my gaze from Mac. My friend ran his hand over his prickly scalp and down the back of his neck before huffing out a long breath. He appeared nervous, and coming from someone who looked like a tank of armor, it couldn't be good.

Standing, I walked over to the living room window, not to look out, but to give myself something to do, because I sensed a missile about to hit its target.

Without turning, I asked, "Why is that, Viper?"

Silence. Patience wore thin as each second trickled by with no answer.

Turning, I caught the end of a stolen glance between Viper and Mac. A secret. My brain might be filled with fog, but I wasn't stupid.

"What's going on?" I held my ground, steadying myself for whatever came.

"Ah, man. I've already told you this once, and it was hard back then. To have to do it again is killing me. I'm just the messenger, okay? So don't shoot me." He moved to the edge of his seat, resting his elbows on his knees, eying me. Unsure.

My blood thickened, slowing down my heartrate to almost nothing as I held my breath.

I glared at him, unable to utter a sound. Whatever he needed to get off his chest weighed a ton. His shoulders sagged as he looked to the ground, then back up.

"The reason you and Trudy split up is because you found out she had been having an affair."

Spine fully extending, I soaked in the words. My wife had cheated? A small sense of betrayal dug a hole in my chest, but simply simmered with no recollection of it. More like a bruised ego hearing it from my friend. The rage I should have felt hadn't stirred yet.

Mac sat in the room, anxiously watching, twirling her wine glass but not drinking.

"Oh? And how did you find out?" It didn't really matter, but I wanted to know.

"I found a letter while on deployment. Trudy sent it."

Confusion had me stare into space to debunk the riddle. How did he find the letter, and had I read it at that stage?

Spinning around to face my friend, I asked, "You read it?" Dumb question. Of course he read it if that's how he found out, but my brain was fuzzy attempting to make sense of something I had no present knowledge of.

Viper shifted uncomfortably. "Only the last page with Trudy's signature."

Striding closer, filtering dozens of questions to get to the most pivotal, I ground out, "What did it say?"

His features took on an anguished guise. He eyeballed me directly. "She declared her love to someone who wasn't you."

I began to get the churning in my gut that I'd come to know preceded something monumental. Viper's face and body were tensing with each passing second, upping my own anger. My friend appeared torn. Jesus! Even with no morsel of memory about the betrayal from my wife, my adrenalin spiked. The air could be cut with a knife. Mac fiddled nervously, not looking at me. Suddenly anger doused my earlier good mood. A hidden part of me wanted to tear someone's head off as I began putting puzzle pieces together. Namely the guy in question, and then I wanted to pay my ex-wife a visit. The letter had never been meant for me. It had been for her lover. A military comrade. Had it been someone on my team? A friend?

Needing clarification on who she had screwed around with, even though I might not recognize the name, I took a deep, centered breath. "Who was it?"

I gave Mac another once-over, needing her comfort. She sat forward on the sofa, biting a fingernail. Clearly she already knew. I'd deal with her later. Right now my laser focus targeted Viper, who lowered his head and gripped the back of his neck.

Not knowing if he'd answer me, I growled, "Who. Was. It?"

Every muscle in me had tightened in preparation. Watching him raise his head, I gathered from the pained expression on his face, I wasn't going to like the answer.

Just when I thought I'd need to shake it out of him, he let one word roll off his tongue. It left Viper and attached itself to me like a living entity.

"Reno."

Chapter Two

Mac

The room fell silent. Shock and tension covered us in a dense blanket so thick, I almost rose and rushed out the front door just so I could breathe again.

It must be hard for Viper to be the bearer of the same bad news twice. Neither of us knew how Harley would react, so I remained focused on him, looking for any sign of a meltdown. So far he had kept it together, and perhaps his limited memory proved a blessing in this instance. Still, with each passing second, his body stiffened further. I could almost hear the cogs of his mind click over. I needed to go comfort him, but I couldn't be sure if he would rebut my attempt, so I remained seated.

"Reno?" he whispered.

"I'm sorry, man. I thought you needed to know before you made any decisions regarding Trudy."

Harley appeared oblivious as he stared through Viper. His mouth stretched tight, his jaw locked.

I wanted to say something, but at the same time, I had no place in doing so.

Viper gave me a troubled look, which I returned. He stood and moved to Harley.

"You okay?" He placed a hand on Harley's shoulder.

Nothing. I'd rather him rant and rave, because then I'd know what he felt. His dazed stupor had me worried.

Viper shook him and Harley found some focus as he lowered himself onto the edge of the coffee table.

"The dream," he murmured, still not completely with us.

"The dream?" queried Viper, bending down so they were at eye level.

"Reno's last words were, 'I'm sorry, man.' I didn't know what it meant when I woke up, but now I do."

"I heard him mumble something but couldn't make it out." Huffing out, Viper continued, "So I'm guessing Trudy decided after Reno's death she would attempt to get back with you. Probably out of guilt."

"I don't remember. I only know what she's told me."

It became obvious Viper didn't like Trudy. His lips sneered at the mention of her. I could see his loyalty to Harley and it comforted me.

"Don't necessarily believe anything that comes out of her mouth. It's convenient for her now that you have amnesia. She could tell you anything and you'd be none the wiser."

"I guess it's settled, then."

I spoke up for the first time. "What?"

Harley finally peered at me. "I won't be moving in with my ex-wife. I'll bunk with Viper for a while. See if we can use his connections to weed out the guy who tried to kill me. Try and find out why I ran solo that night."

I couldn't help the mental high five I gave myself at hearing about Harley not moving in with Trudy. Viper would look out for him and help in any way possible. I could get back to normal and all would be good. A huge part of me would miss having him around, though. Things had subtly changed between us. Perhaps I needed the space from him to think things through.

Some of the responsibility would be taken off me so I could focus on my life. Nick, for instance. He'd have to be dealt with upon his return, but I felt strong enough to lay my cards on the table. I no longer needed comfortable. I no longer wanted mundane. Harley had opened my eyes to that. Even only having met Viper, I could tell he oozed a certain level of danger and fire. The two men sitting in my living room were far from ordinary. To be in the military they obviously craved excitement and liked to live on the edge. Their mindset didn't belong in regular society. Some part of me connected with that. I lived on a razor sharp edge at work, daily, having to make split second decisions that could save or end lives. From the moment I walked through the doors into the hospital, my adrenalin spiked until the second I walked out again.

Being around Harley had propelled that adrenalin in a different way. An intense way. Deep down, I craved it. What would it be like to fully immerse myself in him? To let go of my inhibitions? To surrender to the dark part that lived in us all?

"Mac?"

"Hmm?" I'd zoned right out. Viper had been talking to me and I hadn't heard a word.

"I'm gonna head home now. Nice meeting you." He held out his hand and I shook it vigorously.

"Oh. No problem. Sorry, just thinking about work tomorrow." A lie, but one I seemed to pull off. Viper winked at me and walked with Harley to the door. Clapping each other on the back, I listened as they spoke.

"We'll catch this asshole, bro. Trust me on that. You need a hand getting some stuff from your apartment tomorrow?"

"Nah. I need to hang around here until the alarm's done, and then I'll pick the lock like I did earlier, throw some things into a bag, and head over. Text Mac your address? I need to invest in a new cell."

"Gotcha." Viper fished out his cell, keyed in a few words, and upon hearing the ping of my cell, he pocketed it again.

"Take it easy, man," Harley offered.

"You too. I'll see you tomorrow."

Alone with Harley again, I waited for him to shut the front door and watched as he stalked toward me. His face had hardened into a mask of anger so I kept quiet.

Muscles in his neck threatened to pop as he threw himself down beside me.

"Fuck!" he roared, grabbing his head between his hands and squeezing his scalp.

He had every right to be pissed off. In fact, he'd dealt with everything thus far rather well. If it were me, I'd be a mess right now.

Instead of angering him more by speaking, I rose and filled up his wine glass, knowing he'd need it and more. Not that alcohol should be used as therapy, but I had nothing else to marginally calm him. Except...

Don't go there, Mac. He's vulnerable right now. You need to keep it together. Keep your hands to yourself.

I sat it in front of him on the coffee table, deciding I didn't need any more wine. He slowly raised his head to look at the glass and then to me, his face drawn and tired. Weary from information overload. I could tell he bordered on short-circuiting.

"Drink," I ordered, because what else could I say?

"There's too much shit to process right now," he sighed out, giving me an invitation to talk. His mussed up hair drew my attention for a split second, but I quickly quelled the erotic thoughts bubbling away in my mind. Even with everything that had gone down so far, I could feel the kinetic energy sizzling in the air around us.

"I know. I'm sorry you've had to deal with so much. At least now you know why your marriage failed. Moving in with Trudy would be a mistake."

"It's lucky Viper called you when he did. Perhaps it's all for the best. While I can't remember the clusterfuck of my life, it troubles me that my wife screwed my friend." He swigged the rest of his glass of wine in one swallow, placing it on the coffee table beside me.

"I think moving in with Viper will be good for you, regardless of what you remember."

His stare became intense, causing me to shift slightly.

"You're good for me, Mac. You. Right here. Right now."

Oh no! Retreat! Retreat! When had he edged closer? I had nowhere else to go. The back of my knees were painfully pressed in to the edge of the coffee table. A better question might be, did I truly want him to back off?

Vulnerable, Mac. Remember? My body wasn't listening to logic. It ran its own race.

His heat leached into my pores, causing goosebumps to skitter across my flesh. One man. The only man to ever make me question everything. He had the ability to reconnect my short-circuited nerve endings in such a way, I grappled for oxygen in his presence. His touch scalded. His stare eviscerated me. The 'more' I craved surpassed what I knew I could handle, and yet I wanted nothing more than to push those boundaries of self-control and sensation.

"You with me?" he croaked, his pointer finger running down the ridge of my nose, feather-soft.

I could only minutely nod in my catatonic state. He continued to trace my face while his eyes destroyed me in other ways. I hovered on a cusp of the unknown, torn between freefalling and taking a step back. If I fell there would be no way I'd be able to climb back up, but if I retreated safely, I'd miss the chance to soar. Safety had always been my road in life. I'd never strayed from that. Boring and humdrum. Harley had presented me with an intersection where I could take a risk and turn left into the unknown or remain on the straight and narrow.

I knew what I needed but did I have the strength to chase it? Nick and his neglect came forward into my thoughts, disappointment clinging to it. He couldn't give me what I needed. What I yearned for. I needed to jump off this cliff I teetered on and hope the man in front of me caught me.

You need this, Mac. Live life instead of simply existing. Feel. Discover. Take what you want from a man who will give you everything he has.

Blinking, I inched my mouth closer to his. Time to jump.

Harley must have seen me take the first step because he did catch me as I fell. Without hesitation. Our mouths smashed together, desperate and wild. He dragged me onto his lap where we sank into each other, fully. I feasted on his plush mouth, demanding he give me more by stealing each of his grunts. Large hands gripped my scalp as he pushed himself upward, needing friction. I scooted as far in to his groin as I could, the minute distance still too much.

I sailed on the glorious air current of heady intoxication, surrendering to my descent into the unknown. Freedom gripped me in its clutches in that moment, allowing me to simply *be*.

My chest crushed Harley's, and without even knowing it, I found myself rubbing backward and forward, my nipples rejoicing.

Tearing our mouths apart, Harley's lips swollen from my assault, he rasped, "Jesus. I'm drowning in you, angel, and it's still not enough."

I bit the inside of my cheek as he stood, held my hips to his and walked down the hallway to my room. His strength carried me as if I weighed nothing. His gaze never wavered. I didn't want it to. Anticipation lit the space around us. It seeped from my pores.

Kicking the door shut, he took three strides to the bed and placed me down as if I might break before covering me completely. I saw nothing else. Became nothing else but him. I submerged with him as we drowned in each other.

My cells came alive, kicking me into the stratosphere of want and need. Grasping the bottom of his shirt, I pulled upward, tossing it to the floor so I could bask in Harley's finery. His marked chest drew my mouth forward so I could delicately kiss the wound I had tended. He shivered at the contact, hissing in a breath, not from pain but pleasure.

"It's yours, Mac. Everything. The scar is a tattoo in your honor for saving me. For bringing me back. For finding me when I'd succumbed to the darkness. I wear it with pride."

His words moved me as I continued to trace the outline with my tongue, reveling in the free rein I had.

His skin felt smooth and taut as I moved to his left nipple, gently gripping it with my teeth and pulling. I loved giving in to everything I craved without the fear of rebuttal. Something told me Harley was open to exploring the same facet of myself that existed within him. He relished in my newfound bravado.

"Fuck!" he roared, pushing his pec further into my mouth. "Don't stop."

I loved his reaction, spurring me on to suck hard and then soothe with my tongue, twirling it in between. Each whistle of breath and twitch of his body brought forth my own climbing need. How could I have ever lived without this?

Alternating between both nipples, one hand massaged my neck and shoulders as I tormented him. With a bellow as I bit a tad too hard, we both rolled so I rested on top of him, both his legs parting, allowing me to fall in between. Steady hands ripped my shirt off, and then his open mouth took one of my breasts through the lacy fabric of my bra.

"Ugh. Your tits, woman. A fine feast I'm about to gorge on."

My bra disappeared quicker than my shirt, freeing me to his face. Lifting me upward and in line with his lips, he wasted no time indulging in me. This time I groaned loudly, a zing of electricity rocketing from my nipple to every pleasure point south. He hummed at my response, my body writhing against him.

"Mmm. Look at you, coming alive under my touch. Your nipple is so hard." Flicking it with his tongue, he moved to the other one and ate in a glutinous feast while palming my butt and wrenching me into his hard mass. "There's no going back now, angel. This is happening."

I wouldn't deny him this time. I needed it as much as he did. The way he touched me as if I were a priceless work of art, wrecked me. I came completely undone. His rigid, corrugated abs flexed further under my touch. I dragged my lips from his and lowered myself on a path of erotic destruction by licking and nipping my way to the grand prize. But first I needed to rid him of the intrusive clothing that hindered me from hitting my target. Unzipping his jeans, I shimmied them down his hips, noting the absence of underwear, possibly due to the fact he didn't want to wear Nick's, and marveled at his male perfection jutting skyward. It twitched as I raised my eyes to Harley's, noting the crude way he watched and waited.

The position gave me power. The power to pleasure him while enjoying the fine dining experience. Lowering my mouth to the tip while still eying him, I let my tongue roll out and moisten the head all over, laving around the edges.

The motion pulled a hoarse groan from him, followed by a steady flow of heated bed-talk. "Mmm. Watching that pretty mouth taste me is all kinds of hot. Don't close those stunning eyes. I want to see you take me all the way in. I want every reaction, sound, and emotion from you scorched into my psyche."

God, he was sexy. I couldn't remember who or if anyone had ever had my full attention while giving oral. It opened me up to him and exposed every morsel of desire. I truly came to life.

Fixating on his enlarged pupils, I went to town on his entire length, only losing his sight when I neared the bottom. Angling him toward me, I used my tongue and lips to deliver maximum sensation, loving his strained abdominal muscles and agonized grunts. It brought about my own pleasure, knowing I gave him what he needed.

My mind focused only on him and the way he cherished every lick, suck, and kiss by his sharp intake of breath and tense muscles.

"Keep that up and it will be over real quick," he growled, lifting himself off the pillows to place both his demanding hands underneath my armpits to draw me back up. "As much as I love to watch my hard cock disappear inside those sultry lips, I need more of you."

He didn't have to elaborate. I felt the same. Diving in for a seductive, passionate kiss, I lined myself up over him using my hands. Upon lashing my tongue against his, I lowered my hips down, moaning with bliss as he pierced me, stretching and filling me completely, only minutely taking away the ache to be possessed by him.

"Shit. Shit!" he barked, heaving his hips up, inching that little further so I felt a blissful stab of pleasurable pain. I wailed.

"Harley! Oh God!" I didn't rise up, but ground against him, enjoying the fullness and complete connection as we continued our visual staring session. Everything he felt gazed back at me in his torrid, dark orbs. Like me, he didn't blink much because he didn't want to miss a thing. His constant vocal noises mimicked my own. What I needed, he offered, and what I gave, he took.

Steady fingers found my breasts again, my already engorged beads delighting at the added attention. I couldn't remain still any longer. Everything in me screamed for glorious friction and so I obliged. Resting my hands on his broad chest gave me the leverage I needed to take the reins and ride forcibly, angling myself differently with each thrust downward to discover new sensitive spots inside that had me cry out in wondrous ecstasy.

Harley held firm, enabling me to use him to my advantage. He clearly enjoyed me taking charge.

"This right here. This is everything. You. Me. The connection. There is nothing else, Mac." His hand came to my face. Stroking. Worshipping. I became the Goddess he allowed me to be. The Goddess buried inside who'd never been encouraged to show herself. She simply needed someone to coax her out. The vixen. Life surged through my veins, and for the very first time, I truly felt like *me*.

I rose with the sudden power I had been given and paused before sliding deliciously back down, watching all the tics in Harley's face and neck as he struggled to keep his eyes focused. They glazed over yet remained steady. So sexy.

Cupping both breasts, he kneaded them while tweaking my nipples. Exquisite didn't cover the sensation, but I needed to keep things slow for now to draw out every ounce of pleasure we both had to give.

"Kiss me, angel," he soothed, his tongue moistening both lips.

That mouth. God, that mouth. It beckoned without him having to beg.

Leaning against him, our mouths came together with fierce recklessness while our bodies remained slow and languid. The combination drove me wild, along with the thumping of Harley's heart against my chest. Both of his hands gripped my ass, pulling me harder into his groin in jerky movements. Clearly he struggled to keep his composure.

Tongues and teeth clashed. Lips bruised. Harley held me firm as he took back control, the gentle slide and pull of his cock remaining sensually lazy.

"You feel so good like this," he whispered, only breaking contact momentarily. "I didn't think I'd be able to do slow with you, but I'm loving every second of it."

Him and me both. I'd never done slow with Nick. He'd always gone hell for leather and it was over before it began, due to his 'busy schedule.' To spend the time enjoying another man like this could easily become my new favorite pastime. My sweet addiction.

The build was deliriously slow, but with each thrust from below, I climbed higher on the rung of pleasure.

The 'more' I craved filled not only my body and soul, but the entire room. The man I'd saved had essentially begun to do the same to me. He saved me from the shackles of duty and tedium, leading me to another level of intimacy. There would be no going back from this. No going back from him.

How could I now? I wanted to cry things out. Read him my heart and the words filling it.

"Hey." His thumb pushed into my mouth. "I'm losing you." He stilled below, bringing me back from my head. Biting down on the intrusion, I let my lips glide around it as he pulled it back out.

"No! You're not. I'm here. With you. It's so damn intense, that's all. I've never had this."

Smiling, he sat up so we were still coupled, forcing me to bring my legs around his lower back. "I haven't even begun yet, angel. Whatever you've had in the past? Forget it. My mind might not remember most things, but my body doesn't need a past. It only needs now. It's running on pure instinct. You free me, gorgeous. You let me walk in the present. I don't know what I would have done without you. I need you so much."

The welling of tears had my lip quiver. So sweet. So real and honest. I didn't want to cry. The moment held too many positives to bawl like a baby, even if they were tears of joy.

Swallowing hard, I gave him my own broad grin, feathering over his face lightly with fingers that wanted to steal everything.

"I can't believe you're real. Are you positive I'm not dreaming? Because if I am, I never want to wake up."

For the first time his eyes closed as my fingers danced over his delicate eyelids, feeling the twitching underneath. Still we sat, basking in nothing and everything. Time ticked on, yet stood still as we luxuriated in oblivion.

"I'm real, Mac. Don't ever doubt that. Now, are

we gonna sit here talking all night or am I going to fly you to the stars?"

I shivered. Harley enabled me to grasp those stars. They'd always been so far away, yet he brought them to me with little effort.

"Don't move. Let me move you."

Not sure what he meant, it became clear when he grabbed my hips as if I weighed nothing and began moving me up and down on him while I clung on. Throwing my head back, I couldn't keep my eyes focused. They closed on a wave of delirium as he manipulated me as if I were an instrument and he the musician.

Every downward drag touched a sensitive spot that had me cry out for more...a hidden corner of me no one had ever dared to find.

"Mmm. You like that?" he croaked, bringing his fiery, lush mouth back to my breast, scalding every inch of skin.

"Yes. God, don't stop. Ever."

Chuckling against my nipple, he began to pick up the pace. His throat vibrated with animalistic sounds that rumbled through me. I shuddered once, not quite there yet, but close. His teeth clamped on, sending a buzz of momentary pain outward before it morphed into greedy want as it followed the path to my splayed, open thighs.

He expanded further, stretching me to my limit, creating the push I needed to surge into glory. My breath caught and held, my mind attempting to catch up with my body. Deep within my womb an excruciating bliss-bomb exploded, sending me flying into orbit. My hips bucked and my back arched as I soared.

"I got you," Harley groaned.

And he did. He held me fast with just gentle rocking as a foreign, prolonged sound erupted from my voice box. It appeared as if I suffered, and by God I did. I floated on the very best stream of gratification which reached every hormone-ravaged cell.

More feasting on my breasts held me in nirvana, along with male moans mixed with the scent of orgasm and mild sweat. The combination drove forth more sensation.

"Yeah. That's my girl. Let go and feel how good it is. Fall and I'll catch you."

His words egged me on as I continued to climax, not knowing how he held his own release at bay. Every tense muscle in me became pliant and droopy and I let go of everything holding me prisoner.

"Show me your eyes," he commanded.

My head flopped forward until we found each other. I could barely keep my lids from closing as I quaked and shook.

Even though I drifted, as I looked at him again, we flew together. I burned for him, and the way his dark pupils fully expanded in lust, I knew he held onto his control by a thread. His body brought me freedom but his eyes captured everything else as he let me in to see the deepest part of him. A window into the man who'd lost everything, yet in our intimate moment, appeared to have found what he'd always been looking for. I knew because it mirrored my own incredible revelation. We'd found ourselves in each other.

Waiting for my crashing wave to recede, he lowered us to the bed and flipped us again so he was on top. Pushing my knees up high and spreading me further apart, I noticed a flick switch in his demeanor.

"My turn." Kissing the inside of my upper leg, he towered over me, all primed, gleaming muscle, ready for battle.

I could do nothing but nod, accepting his onslaught, which I knew would destroy me, totally.

There was no easing into it. He had passed the point of slow and gone straight to annihilate.

Heaven have mercy. I wouldn't be able to walk tomorrow at work.

He snarled as he pummeled me into the mattress, my dwindling orgasm having not totally disappeared. My nerve endings still sparked and ignited to flames once more.

His eyes flashed from mine to where he plowed in and out. He sucked in air through his open mouth in between cusses and grunts. His nipples were as hard as mine, the veins in his neck protruding, bracketing each side of the rigid column.

He let go a howl, locking on to my half-shut eyes and flaying open his very soul while he thrust hard once. Twice. Three times, before stilling as scorching magma spilled inside me, spurring a rolling climax to rocket out of nowhere as my cervix contracted once more.

Smothering me with his shaking physique, he murmured in my ear, "Don't leave me."

Again with the 'don't leave me' plea. He had issues with abandonment I hoped we could sort out.

I needed to assure him of my intentions.
"I'm not going anywhere, I promise."

Chapter Three

Harley

I never wanted to let her go. The woman had me. All of me. Resting in a tangled mess of limbs, I listened to her quiet breathing, unable to fall asleep. Her bedside clock read 11 p.m. Our hot session hadn't ended with sex, but had continued in the form of feathery touches and soft kisses. The reality of making love to Mac differed greatly from my fantasies. Her trust in me and the way she gave herself over to her feelings blew my mind. We'd clicked together and locked into place like some laser-cut key and keyhole.

She'd seen me vulnerable and open, and I, her. We'd both totally thrown our guards down, the sensation liberating. Like she now knew me, better than I knew myself: a man with no past. That, in itself, freed me.

My hand rested on her stomach as I lay on my side watching the way her lips had fallen apart and her hair fanned out a knotty mess on the pillow. She

27

took my breath away.

I didn't want to leave her to move in with Viper. It would make her vulnerable. Perhaps I'd discuss her moving in with my friend and I. At least until the assailant who'd attacked me had been either killed or arrested. An alarm being fitted to her apartment didn't necessarily mean she'd remain safe. I couldn't keep an eye on her while I wasn't here.

The thought of anything happening to her soured my stomach. In a short time my feelings for her had escalated into something vast. Maybe even love. I wouldn't tell her that though. She still had to deal with her ex. The way she'd cherished me with her eyes and body earlier had me hoping she felt the same or at least enough to keep seeing me.

Sometime in the small hours of morning, I must have dozed off, because the next thing I knew the bedroom light had been switched on and a loud voice cried out, "What the hell? You have got to be kidding me!"

I sat upright and Mac stirred, rubbing her bleary eyes. The sky lightened outside. Turning to the male voice, I cursed, seeing Nick standing in the doorway, bag in hand, fury on his face.

The moment Mac turned and realized who stood before us she gasped and drew the sheet tighter around her.

"Nick! What are you doing here? I mean, it's barely morning!"

"I live here, remember?" he roared. "And what the hell is he still doing here? In our bed! Naked! Jesus, Mac!" Dropping his bag, he scrubbed a hand over his face before stalking toward me.

"You! Get the fuck out of my bed and my house! Now! You son of a bitch. You moved right in on my girlfriend the moment I left. How convenient I had to leave town."

There were so many things I wanted to say, but it really wasn't my place. Rising stark naked, I threw on some boxers—some of Nick's boxers—and stalked into the kitchen, giving him a leer as I pushed past. Mac needed to speak with the guy alone. I prayed she had the strength to kick him to the curb or tell him she'd had enough. Closing the door to give them privacy, I tamped down my guilt that I had caused all of this. It hadn't been my intention. If Mac had been happy with her boyfriend I would have backed the fuck off, but 'blind Freddy' could see her misery.

While I switched on the coffee pot and sat at the table, raised voices echoed down the hallway. I tried not to listen, catching only a few words at a time.

"never home…work…sick of it…"

"…cheating…us…him…"

If things got too heated, I'd have no choice but to step in to protect Mac. Until then I needed to have faith she could handle it on her own. As much as Nick seemed like a straight-laced executive type, who knew what he'd do if pushed.

Damn. She didn't need this. I'd been too hasty in throwing myself at her. Maybe I did need to leave and trust that Nick would keep her safe. Letting the idea float in my sleep-deprived brain, I rebutted it. Like hell he could keep her safe. His work came first. He didn't look the type to be able to protect her, let alone himself, regardless of his current anger. No. I'd stand by my pledge to keep her unharmed at all costs.

When drawers and doors began slamming, my hands gripped the edge of the table, preparing to act. My soldier instincts whispered to me that a possible threat loomed, my feet were flat on the floor, ready to kick off and run.

The bedroom door swung open, the sound of the handle hitting the plasterboard, followed by heavy footsteps and more drawers and cupboards being opened and closed.

"I can't be with someone who puts work first, regardless of why you do it. Don't you see that? So many times, we arranged to spend time together only to have you cancel. I'm sick of it."

"Oh you're sick of it? How about being more understanding about what I want or need? I work *for* you. For our future. A little understanding would go a long way to supporting me."

"This conversation keeps repeating itself. I don't care about the future. I care about the now. And at present I'm not getting anything from this relationship. Nothing."

"So you jump into bed with a stranger? Who are you, Mac? The girl I met never would have considered that."

"The girl you met has changed. The girl you met found out she needed more!" Mac's voice was shrill with frustration.

"Oh, and you think he can give you that?" *Watch it, asshole.* My ears burned. *Damn straight I can give her that, you selfish prick.*

"It's not about Harley. It's about us. We've grown so far apart I can't see you anymore."

"Whatever. I know when I'm not wanted. I'll get my name taken off the lease. Here. Give lover boy these keys. I'm sure he'll be needing them."

More footsteps. I had my back to the opening of the living room. The shoes neared and then stopped nearby. I daren't look because I knew I'd say something I'd regret. After a pause, they padded across the carpet and exited the house. The front door banging shut shook the walls.

As soon as his car screeched off, I rose and hurried to Mac.

I found her face down on the bed, sobbing.

"Hey. Do you want me to leave?"

She didn't answer but merely shook her head. Did I go to her or give her some time? Remembering Nick's absence when she'd needed him, I strode over to the bed and lay down beside her, stroking the back of her head.

"I'm so sorry, angel."

"I don't even know why I'm crying," she choked out. "I'm relieved he's gone, but at the same time, I feel sick about him seeing us together. I didn't want it to be like that. I wanted to sit down and talk to him. I at least owed him that."

"I know. But you weren't to know he'd arrive unannounced."

"Still, we shouldn't have slept together until after it was over with Nick. I feel like such a bitch."

"Shhh. You're far from a bitch. You're an amazing, intelligent, sexy woman who has needs. He wasn't taking care of you."

"It doesn't make it right, though."

"No, it doesn't, but maybe it's for the best."

She turned her head to face me, her tear-streaked face breaking my already fragile heart. Feathering my fingers over her cheeks, catching the new droplets, I did my best to offer comfort. "It's all on me. I take full responsibility. None of this is your fault. You did your best to push me away. I should have respected your situation and avoided any physical contact. I tried. I really did, angel, but the pull to you won out in the end. I can't stop it. It's too strong."

She stared at me, letting me pet her, leaning in to my touch. God, this woman had been so starved for affection of any kind. I hated that bastard Nick for depriving her of a basic human need.

His selfish actions had ended the relationship long before I came along. My arrival merely opened Mac's eyes to how much she'd missed out on.

"Whatever you need, it's yours. I'm here for you."

Giving me a half-smile, she said, "Thank you. This isn't your fault. I brought you home. I let myself feel something for you. I don't want you bearing the burden of my problems."

"Let's agree that we're both to blame then and leave it at that." Kissing her forehead, I sat up. "Coffee?"

"Mmm, thanks. I need to rise anyway and get ready for work. I'll have a quick shower and meet you in the kitchen."

"Sounds good." Leaning down again, I found her mouth and gave her a soft, lingering kiss before moving away to pour us both a large hit of caffeine.

Chapter Four

Mac

What had I done? Easing into the shower with Harley's scent covering me, I let the spray wash it away. I felt cheap and embarrassed. Not because Harley made me feel so good, but because Nick had returned home and caught us. I should have ignored my body's craving for a man's touch. Knowing Nick would be home any day, I lost myself in my John Doe. I deserved the shame and humiliation. I'd never meant it to end that way.

Why did Harley have to be so darn tempting? My will crumbled in his company. He had an energy I couldn't ignore. Last night...holy cow. Hot didn't begin to cover it. Even with my conscience chastising me for the way things ended with Nick, my essence cried out for the stranger I'd brought into my home.

Should I deny myself the chance to nourish my soul with his power and presence? It wasn't fair on Nick to remain with him when I craved what he couldn't give me. He deserved a partner who accepted his hectic work schedule and odd hours. There had to be someone out there who fit his mold.

Switching the water off, I dried and dressed in my spare scrubs, tying my hair up in its necessary bun for work and slipping into my flats.

The smell of strong coffee drew me down the hallway, my stomach tipping when I spied Harley with his back to me at the table, sipping from a mug, clad only in boxers.

Broad shoulders were the gateway to a carved back, refined in every way. I'd clung to his adequate expanse the night before, kneading the bulk and relishing in its density. My fingers twitched with an itch to scratch and claw, but I held back, the echo of my self-reproach mulling in my brain.

Noting my mug placed opposite him, I sat, giving my attention to my steaming coffee, wishing I could immerse myself and disappear into the brown liquid.

"Hey," he muttered.

When I didn't respond, he half-stood and leaned over the table, setting his hand on the juncture of my neck and shoulder so he could swipe his thumb against the underside of my jaw.

"You overthinking things?"

With his touch marking me with kindness, I had no choice but to give him my full focus.

"I guess. Just feeling shitty about everything."

"Don't. Everything will be okay. Things happen for a reason. What went down forced you to address your relationship with Nick. Sometimes the universe has a way of giving us nudges to urge us along."

Floundering under his perusal, I acknowledged his wisdom as the truth, attempting to use it to smother my guilt. With a slight nod and a forced smile, he reclined back into his chair, giving me space to breathe.

While I sipped, he spoke. "I've been doing some thinking and I have a proposition for you."

Christ. A proposition? Now? After the fiasco this morning? I couldn't handle any more decisions today.

"Harley…" I began, but didn't get a chance to finish.

"Wait. Before you say anything, hear me out. I realize your alarm is meant to be fitted tomorrow, but in all honesty, I question just how much it will keep you safe. Viper's arrival has changed things. I feel if you were to move into his place with me, we could almost guarantee no harm would come to you."

What? Just up and go? What about the apartment? Nick had left. I couldn't just vacate and leave it empty. I'd still be required to pay the lease. Or find someone to take over the payments. Plus, did I really want to move in with two males? And had Viper agreed to this? What about Harley needing to leave to keep me safe?

"Look. I know you mean well, but this is my home. What would I do with all my stuff? Who would I get to move in here?"

"Advertise. It's close to the heart of town and public transport. I don't think you'd have to worry about it staying empty for long."

"And the alarm?"

"I can call and cancel it today while you're at work."

Gah! Things were moving too quickly. I couldn't process it all. Suddenly my world had been turned on its axis and I dangled precariously upside down.

I couldn't argue with the fact that Viper and Harley could keep me safe. That didn't factor into it, but if they were going to be guarding me constantly, my freedom would be robbed. At least here, inside, I had my own space. Was I really in so much danger I warranted a permanent guard?

"Plus, having you with me would give me peace of mind. I don't know what those mongrels are capable of, but I have a feeling they're watching and waiting to strike again. They almost killed me, Mac. I don't want you to suffer the same fate."

His argument played with my instincts to remain safe. Would they really hurt me? I hated the idea of being in danger. Unknowingly I may have put a target on my head the moment I stepped into the ICU room housing the handsome stranger with a dark, yet obscure past. What if his attackers knew where I worked? Surely if they'd found my place of residence, it would be easy to track me to University Hospital.

"I never wanted any of this. I just wanted to make a difference and live my life." I sighed it out, focused on Harley's reaction.

"I hear you, angel. I had no idea about the shit that would find me. I don't want you involved in my fucked up life, but the fact is, now that I've dragged it to your doorstep, it's my job to protect you and keep you safe. Let me do that. Please? I couldn't save Reno…"

Pain glittered in his eyes and clarity washed over me. Losing his friend even though he'd since learned of his betrayal, cut him deeply. He didn't want to lose me the same way.

"What about my apartment?" Again I asked the question. I had work today. I didn't have time to search for a tenant.

"I'll get Viper to ask his contacts. If nothing comes of it, we'll place an ad. Don't worry, it won't be vacant for long."

I knew I could regret my decision, but on a whim, I blurted out, "Fine. Only until the bastards are caught."

Squeezing my eyes shut tightly, I heard his chair push back and then his nearness enveloped me. Chancing a peek, I found him kneeling on the floor beside me, scraping my chair on the floor as he turned me to face him.

With so much sincerity, he gripped my thighs and drilled me fiercely with two fathomless lasers. "Good girl. You've made the right choice. I promise you here and now that I will do everything in my power to protect you. So will Viper."

The steadfast vow chipped away at my will, warming every corner of my insides. Hearing his oath made me believe that perhaps he could stay true to his word.

Sagging against the back of the chair, I relaxed a bit. "Thank you. I'll go pack a bag and you can drop me off at work and then pick me up this afternoon.

We can head straight to Viper's. Make sure it's okay with him, though."

"Already done, sweet cheeks." He beamed. "He's all for it. This was my plan B."

I wasn't sure what I had got myself into, but I would soon find out.

Chapter Five

Harley

Thank God for small mercies. Mac agreeing to move in with Viper and me relaxed me somewhat. I didn't think she'd concede so fast, but self-preservation had won her over. And so it should. No one liked the idea of a possible threat looming over their heads. This way, she had not one protector, but two.

Come hell or high water, any demented fuck who dared mess with us and used Mac to do it would pay with their life. Fool me once, shame on you. I would be prepared. While my angel worked her pretty ass off today, I planned on getting a locksmith out to my apartment to cut a key and then I'd scour the place for any and all weapons I could take to Viper's. There had to be some cash lying around I'd failed to see last time I visited, but I'd turn the place over if I had to.

First order of the day—getting my girl to work.

My girl. Had I laid claim to her? I guess the

moment I vowed to put my own life above hers and kill to protect her, yes, she had become mine.

All five foot six of her. Stubbornness and all.

"You ready?" I called from the living room where I'd been lacing up my black boots. Just one of the items I'd packed from my place and brought to Mac's. My stonewashed jeans I'd worn yesterday hung low and comfortable, a navy tee hiding my scarred chest.

"Yep. Go start the car. I'll be out in a sec!" she sang from the bedroom.

A comfortable feeling settled deep within me. As if Mac and I had been together forever. The idea of me driving her to work felt normal. Slowly I began forging a new life after my attack, learning to live with what I had. I'd been given a second chance and I sure as heck wasn't going to waste it. Evil had tried to destroy me, but failed. I might not know much, but I knew next time I would fight to the death.

Opening the garage door, I fired up Mac's Mustang, loving her chunky growl. Who would have thought an ICU nurse would own such a fine piece of machinery? She rumbled and vibrated as I waited another minute before Mac appeared.

Name badge in place and purse under her arm, she climbed in beside me, grinning.

"What?"

"My car suits you. I called you Harley because I thought you looked like you rode a bike, but after seeing you behind the wheel of my girl, I'm reconsidering the moniker."

Laughing, I had to ask, "Oh? And what would

you change my name to?"

Thinking about it, as I idled out and shut the door, she answered, "Ford."

"Hahahaha!" I barked, "Ford? That's not even a name."

"Sure it is. I know a guy called Ford."

"What does he drive?"

"A Toyota."

I roared at that and Mac joined in too. The sound of her laughter lifted me higher. She still chuckled as she quickly pointed out her window. "Turn left here. Sorry, I forgot you don't know where you're going."

"That's right. You could say, I'm new to town." I slanted her a smirk.

She smiled. "Do you think you'll ever go back to the name Declan?"

"Doubtful at this stage. I prefer Harley."

"Why is that?"

"Because you gave it to me. You gave me an identity."

She looked down, embarrassed. "It only began as an alternative to John Doe. When you woke up with amnesia, it just stuck."

"Harley is who I am now. Declan lived in my invisible past. There's no going back." I took comfort in that. My present existed with Mac. It's all I had and all I wanted. Snatching her hand up from her lap, I laced our fingers, squeezing.

"Turn right!" she yelped, right before I startled and slammed on the brakes.

***

After dropping Mac off in the staff parking lot, which she had access to via a card she handed me so I could pick her up at the end of the day, I drove back to Mac's first and called Viper from her landline, and then retraced the route to my apartment. My friend agreed to meet me there.

It proved to be a roundabout way, but until I knew the town inside out, I could only travel where I had been before.

I had to learn everything over again, which proved time-consuming, but I had no choice if I wanted to live a normal life again.

My apartment wasn't too far from Mac's, and when I arrived, Viper already stood out front. A van with Keyed-Up Locksmiths painted on the side had parked in front of my garage, so I turned right and drove to the nearest visitor space, making sure to lock the 'Stang up.

"Hey man. We just got here."

"You fly here?" I joked, nodding to the guy who had his back to me, bent over my front door handle.

"My place is only a couple of minutes away. This dude I called was on his way to another job but I offered to pay him double, so he squeezed you in."

Shaking my head at Viper, I barked, "You do realize I have to foot the bill, don't you? I'm not letting you pay."

"Shut it, dude. I got this. That's what friends are for. You can come to my rescue another time."

Not arguing, I nodded and we waited while the locksmith strolled to his van, slid the side door open, and proceeded to cut my new key.

It would be good to be able to enter my place

legally, without having to break in. I could come and go as I pleased.

Making small talk, I mentioned, "Do you know anyone who'd take over Mac's lease? There will be no one paying it until someone is found."

Pausing, he shrugged. "I'll check around. Ask some of the guys."

"Thanks. We'll need to get her stuff moved out before that happens."

"Just give me a time and I'll be there." He slugged me on the back a couple of times, cementing his vow.

From the little I knew of my friend, I knew his word was gospel. Another instinctual feeling. To have had my back in battle proved good enough.

We were interrupted by the locksmith, who handed Viper a key, who then handed it to me. Pulling his wallet out of his pocket, he handed the guy two one hundred dollar bills. "Thanks for fitting us in."

Smiling, the overpaid dude folded the notes and put them into his shirt pocket. "No drama. Call again if you get stuck."

I'll bet. Getting paid double would entice me too.

When he left, I stalked to my door, inserting the key, and pushing it open. "You seriously paid the guy two hundred dollars for a key? You obviously have way too much money."

He followed me in. "Being on missions most of the time means I earn, but don't spend. I've got enough cash to live on for the rest of my life if I so choose. Same goes for you, bro."

Spinning to face him, I let my eyebrows lift in

question. "What are you talking about?"

"Follow me." He chuckled, striding through my small kitchen and into the bedroom.

Not knowing what he meant, I followed, watching as he dragged my bed diagonally, stooping down to remove a piece of carpet which had been cut into a segment no more than two foot square. Underneath the carpet, he lifted a hunk of wood which fitted into the concrete slab and then grinned at me.

"I might need some help with this. She's a heavy bitch."

"What the fuck?"

Closing the gap, I stopped and peered down into the hole, to find a slightly smaller metal box sitting pretty.

"A safe?" I asked, dumbfounded.

"Yep. She's full too." Seeing my perplexed expression, he added, "Don't worry. I'm the only one who knows about it. You entrusted me with the knowledge should I need to remove it in a hurry if you weren't around."

Gripping the back of my neck, I breathed out hard. "Jesus. This would have come in handy the past week or so. Mac's been paying for everything."

"Now you know. Help me lift her up."

Bending down, we both gripped two corners each and heaved. He wasn't kidding when he said it weighed a ton.

"One question. Why do I have a full safe embedded in the floor of my bedroom?"

"We're military ghosts. We all have them. Technically, we don't exist. It just makes things easier."

Placing the safe on the floor, I stepped back. "Okay, genius. We have the thing out. How do you propose we open it when I can't even remember owning the damn thing?"

Turning the round dial on the front, he shot me a quick glance. "You gave me the code. You know. In case. Looks like now you'll be glad you did."

Smart ass. He exuded cocky. I couldn't reprimand him though, because without him, I'd be penniless.

A few left and right turns and the heavy door swung open, revealing stacks of hundred dollar bills piled to the top.

"The pot of gold, my man. The pot of gold."

Grabbing a stack of notes, I let the feel of it sink into my skin. I had a shitload of money.

"I'm gathering we get paid well for our jobs?"

"Oh yeah. We're looked after. You'll never have to worry about money again, let's put it that way."

I didn't doubt it as I stared at the pile, shaking my head at the irony of it all.

"Leave the safe here and stow the money in a bag. I've got two bigger babies at my place. You can use one. Saves lugging this sucker out."

"Good point." I stood, and remembering a large bag in my closet space, I walked over and retrieved it, stacking the money inside. "Anything else I should know, like where my weapons are?"

"You used to carry your MK23 on your person, but I'm assuming when you were ambushed, it got stolen."

"Shit. So I have nothing?"

"I can gear you up, man. Don't worry about it. Just pack clothes and necessities, and let's get out of here."

Throwing some shirts, shorts, jeans, shoes, and a couple of jackets on top of my wad of cash, I grabbed a few toiletries and scanned the apartment for anything else of use. I truly didn't have too much, apart from the cash. If I wasn't home much, it made sense.

"All ready." I nodded to Viper.

"You follow me in Mac's car. We can pick up your truck tomorrow." Looking at me weird, he asked, "Uhh, you do have a set of spare keys to it, right? Or do I have to call the locksmith again?"

"Shit." I couldn't remember. "Let me check the glove compartment."

Walking to the garage, I opened the passenger door and checked everywhere. Nothing. Heading back inside, I opened drawers, checking in my bedroom and the kitchen, but came up empty.

"Damn it. Looks like I will be forking out for a new key. Not today though. I'm sure Mac won't mind me driving her beast for the next day or two."

"Okay. Let's head out then. See you soon."

Hopping into the Mustang, I followed Viper the short distance to his house. We all lived relatively close to each other, which proved to be an asset.

Thoughts morphed to Mac as I drove. I wound my window down to let in fresh air, banging my fingers on the steering wheel in time to a random song on the radio.

Last night had blown my mind. And my groin. Literally. Damn, she had pulled every ounce of pleasure from me. I hardened just reliving our explosive evening. She'd been every bit as sensual as I'd imagined. Now that I had her, I couldn't let her go. Didn't want to. Ever.

If we began a committed relationship, would she cope with me being away often? More to the point, did I even want to return to the military? Surely if my memory never returned fully, I'd be deemed unfit for duty. What other jobs could I do? Security perhaps?

For whatever reason my ex-wife had turned to Reno for attention, I vowed, I wouldn't let the same happen to Mac. I wouldn't make the same mistake twice.

Parking in the driveway, Viper kept his garage door open until I was out with my packed bag and inside before closing it. Nothing about his house seemed familiar. He stopped and let me take it all in before asking, "Bring back any memories?"

"Nah. Not yet."

"Well, make yourself at home. You want a beer?"

"Is the sky blue?"

Laughing, he moved to the fridge and removed a couple of beers, handing me one. I sat on a comfortable dark brown, leather recliner, placing my bag on the floor next to the side table. Viper took the other one. We were quiet and in our own thoughts for a beat too long before the silence broke.

"You gonna call your mom?" Viper's question spiraled me out of my own head instantly.

"Huh?"

"Your mom. Don't you think you should at least call her?"

"And say what, exactly? Hi, Mom. It's your son. I'd love to come visit but I can't exactly remember who the fuck you are?"

His eyebrows raised slightly, but other than that, he remained neutral.

"She'll understand if you explain what happened. She's still your mom, regardless. You were close to her. I think you need to make contact and fess up. For her sake, not yours."

I took his advice on board, putting myself in my mother's shoes. My dad had died and I worked in a job fraught with danger. She must worry.

Resting my head back on the seat, I let a deep breath out. "You're right. I've gotta stop being a self-absorbed ass and just do it. Maybe tomorrow."

"Pfft. Yeah, maybe tomorrow."

"What's that supposed to mean?"

"I've heard hundreds of 'maybe tomorrows.' Just hope you do."

Would I call? Part of me wanted to and the other part knew how much it would hurt her. How could I look at the woman who gave birth to me and not feel a thing? As much as I stayed detached from my past, I wasn't enough of an asshole to not be affected by the grief she would suffer. Could I put her through that, or would staying away and not contacting her hurt more?

"If you want to visit, I'll go with you. She loves me," Viper admitted a tad too cockily.

I connected with his blue eyes, noting the gleam in them.

"You goad me?" I scoffed.

Snorting, Viper, swigged his beer. "No goading. Just simple facts. Your fine mother happens to think the sun shines out of my butt."

"Is that so? Well, after meeting you, I'm beginning to think my mom is an extremely poor judge of character," I joked.

"Hey dick. Watch it. I can't be too bad. You chose me to be best man at your wedding."

My wedding. More like a sham. The idea of it all being for nothing sat heavy on my chest.

Not wanting to talk about Trudy or the things she'd done, I changed the subject. "You live here alone?"

"Ah, yeah. No girlfriend at the moment."

"What I mean is, you don't strike me as the low-set suburban house type of guy."

Tossing me a brief scowl, he said, "It's a story for another day. Let's just say it was going to be a family home."

Oh. As much as I wanted to, I didn't go there. His facial expression told me to leave it alone.

The place danced with light through floor to ceiling open windows and warm colors via the furnishings. A wall mounted television hung opposite. Aside from that, the space appeared uncluttered and clean.

Rising from his chair and placing his can of beer on the coffee table, he offered, "Make yourself at home. I'm gonna take a shower. Your room's the last door down the hallway on the left."

"Thanks, man. I appreciate this."

"I got your back, always." He grinned, walking

off.

Realistically, I should know where to find everything, but my reality had been severely altered, so it became a case of re-learning a lot. Following Viper's instructions, I found a small, tidy room with a double bed, closet, and full-length window looking out over the decent-sized yard.

It would do for my stay. Viper needed to work with me, and hopefully military intelligence, to find the fucker or fuckers who had jumped me and left me for dead.

None of us would be safe until that happened. I wanted blood, and I'm sure Viper did too, so with his superior knowledge and contacts, I'd let him lead the race. Due to my current circumstances, I could only follow.

We spent the better part of the day chatting while enjoying another beer or two. Viper did most of the talking as he recounted stories of old. Our time doing tours and the fun times while back home. He didn't mention any more about why he'd purchased a family house, so I let it go. He'd bring it up when he wanted to. It appeared we'd done a lot together, and the more stories I heard, the greater my respect for the guy sitting beside me.

He retold his heartache at his parents' passing, and as an only child, he had no one close by. Relatives were scattered around the country. I felt sorry for him being alone and wondered if that was the reason he'd wanted me to move in. He thought of me like a brother.

Handing me a blank card, I stared at the cell number, looking up with raised eyebrows.

"My private number. In case you need it. Don't give it to anyone."

"Thanks." Shoving it into the pocket of my jeans, I didn't give it another thought, happy I'd be able to call him should I need to, even though I didn't own a cell. I'd rectify that tomorrow.

The time powered on and before I knew it, the end of the day had neared. Mac needed to be picked up from work, so I threw my boots back on and headed out, remembering the route to the hospital.

It bustled as usual, a parking space hard to find in the staff area. Driving around and around four times, I eventually spotted a car reversing out and nabbed it before anyone else did.

An ambulance blared its siren and tore into the emergency entrance, another victim unknowingly impinging on an already overcrowded system. I knew from my time here, nurses and doctors were overworked due to staff shortages, many of them doing back to back shifts. A little disconcerting to have the welfare of sick patients being tended to by exhausted physicians.

Entering the building and heading toward ICU, I buzzed on the intercom and waited for someone to address me.

"Hello, how can we help?"

"Hi. I'm here to pick up Mackenzie Nichols. She works in intensive care."

"One moment and I'll let her know. Take a seat, please."

A couple of people already waited to go through to see loved ones. Generally they only allowed one at a time due to the critical nature of the patients. I'd learned a lot from Mac about how the ICU operated.

A large wall-mounted television with the volume barely audible played a news channel so I watched without really seeing, hating the feel the hospital gave me. The smell. The sounds. Both associated with sickness and death. Or in my case, losing my past. A small chill rattled up my spine, but it passed quickly.

My foot tapped on the floor in a nervous melody to an invisible tune. Would Mac be staying back late? Shit. I hoped not. I needed to get out of here as soon as possible.

I craved to see her again. It had only been eight hours, but it felt so much longer. She could definitely become my latest addiction. One I don't think I'd ever get over. Moving her in felt right in so many ways, not just the 'keeping her safe' one. I wanted her around. To get to know her more. I'd only scratched the surface of her depth and I couldn't wait to uncover more.

After ten minutes of sitting, getting antsy, I rose and pressed the intercom button again.

"Hello?"

"Yeah, I'm still waiting on Mackenzie, the nurse. I need to know if she's working back, or finishing up."

The female voice sounded the same as earlier. "There's someone looking for her now. Shouldn't be too much longer."

Coming from a staff member in a hospital, I knew it could be ages.

Sitting back down, I flipped through a boating magazine, eying the expensive, gleaming water-cruisers, thinking of how nice it would be to sail away with Mac and forget about the rest of the world. Just the two of us. No drama. No stress. No potential killers lurking. Just the ocean, sky, and our naked bodies writhing on the deck under the sun. Yeah, that sounded nice. Perhaps tonight we could re-create the 'bodies writhing' part. We'd need to keep it quiet under Viper's roof. The way Mac sounded out her release last night, there'd be no hiding what we were up to.

The door opened beside the intercom and I sat straighter, expecting my stunning blonde to walk through, but it was a male doctor who called out a name. One of the visitors near me got up and walked through, the door shutting again.

How long did it take to find a nurse in ICU? It wasn't that big. Maybe she'd gone to a different ward or had to take blood to pathology. I hated waiting.

The door opened again and this time a dark-haired nurse exited, eying me and the other visitor before she stopped and asked, "Who's here for Mackenzie?"

Raising my hand like a five year old, I said, "Me."

She frowned. "We're still trying to locate her. She should have been back from her break an hour ago. She missed lunch, so she went to the staff canteen to grab a coffee and apparently no one's seen her since."

I stood, towering over the poor nurse like a Phoenix rising from its ashes. "What do you mean no one's seen her since? It's a busy hospital. How can that be?"

"I'm sorry, sir, but if you want to hang around we can look into it more."

Niggles of anxiety sizzled in my bloodstream until full-blown fear cemented itself behind my ribs, deep within my chest cavity. A nurse couldn't vanish. Especially Mac. She wouldn't walk out or abandon her job. Unless…fuck!

Chapter Six

Mac

The staff cafeteria contained nurses and doctors like me who'd forgone lunch and were grabbing a quick hit of caffeine to last them the rest of the day. Choosing not to wait in line, I continued to the ground floor to the public cafeteria, knowing Ruth would be serving. She always let me go behind the counter to make myself a 'real' coffee, should I get sick of the instant variety served upstairs, or if I didn't want to wait in line like this afternoon.

Walking down a long corridor to the bank of elevators, I turned to scan the empty area behind me as pinpricks of flesh bubbled all over. An impression of being watched crept along my spine, unsettling me. I could still hear chatter from the nurses' station not far away seeping through the walls, so trying not to worry, I increased my pace.

There weren't many parts of the hospital that creeped me out, apart from the morgue for obvious reasons, so the increasing discomfort I had now made me jittery. Turning right, I relaxed slightly as the elevators came into view. Perhaps my nerves were still frayed after the break-in at my apartment.

Stopping in front of the elevator, I pressed the down button and found the car already there. Stepping in, I turned to wait for the doors to shut. Just as they were about to, a doctor came flying around the corner, calling out, "Nurse! Wait!"

Having seen many a frantic doctor racing through hallways, I knew it must be urgent, so I pressed the button to hold the doors open for him.

I hadn't seen him before, but that didn't mean much. New doctors, interns, and surgeons were brought in regularly, making it virtually impossible to keep up with.

Smiling, I asked, "Are you new here?" The doors closed, slowly.

"Yes." His curt voice had me take pause, briefly turning to check if he had a name tag.

None.

Suddenly the air in the elevator evaporated, leaving me with the same uneasy sensation I'd experienced in the corridor. The dark-haired doctor stood too close. Before I could move away, he leaned down to me and whispered, "We're going to the basement. You're not going to scream, move, or look at anyone else who enters. Understood?"

Alarm shooting through me, I nodded without thinking.

"If you make a sound or attempt to run, I will shoot whoever is in my path." Pulling his blue medical shirt up, he showed me a black handgun tucked into the waist band of his scrubs.

My heart plummeted at the same speed as the elevator. I didn't know what to do. Fear made me remain mute as the bell dinged, signaling the arrival on the ground floor. As the doors opened and five people strolled on board, none the wiser, I felt a hand bunch my own scrubs at the back and pull me backward to make room. It stayed there, informing me to honor my vow to keep quiet.

Why me? What did he want? Rationale attempted to break through my haze in order to figure out how to escape a man who'd clearly lost the plot. My instincts were to call his bluff and run like hell before the doors closed, but needing to keep everyone else in the vicinity safe overpowered all else.

Quiet chatter trickled through the car. A couple smiled at each other, oblivious to the man with a gun standing directly behind them. An elderly woman beside him, watched the light on the wall signal our arrival to the basement as we jerked slightly and stopped. My chest ached, adrenalin pouring to my muscles. I knew once I stepped out of the confines of the elevator, the true terror would begin. My assailant moved forward, banging into the happy couple, who gave him contemptuous glares while he gripped my arm and dragged me out. My feet didn't want to move. Every flight or fight response I owned had been tripped to high alert. The sound of the door closing echoed loudly in the quiet of the basement, like my world rose with the five strangers, leaving me in a new reality. One which reeked of hell.

My voice found me finally. "Who are you? Why

are you doing this? Where are we going?"

Still clutching my arm tightly, he increased the pressure, causing me to suck in a sharp breath.

"Don't speak or I'll shoot you right here."

I really didn't expect him to explain himself. Someone who took another at gunpoint wasn't exactly going to chat about the why's of it all. He had an agenda and it didn't involve me asking questions.

I needed to keep my head in the game even though my stomach roiled and acid rose to my throat, threatening to upend its contents all over the concrete.

I needed to watch and wait for him to let his guard down just a tiny bit and use it to my advantage to escape. I had no other option.

Stopping at a black, heavily tinted SUV, he unlocked the doors and pushed me into the passenger seat via the driver's side, whereby I had to scramble across the center console while he aimed the gun at me so I wouldn't do anything stupid like try to escape.

As he climbed in beside me, blood roared in my ears. Getting in the car had almost sealed my fate, but I'd had no choice. My life or the lives of other innocents. I never wanted to die a martyr, but if it came down to it, I would. To keep others safe. I'd never have chosen to become a nurse if that weren't the case.

We reversed and eased out of the parking lot like two regular people, heading back to normality after visiting a sick friend or relative. We passed nurses beginning their shifts and all I wanted to do was bang on the window to get their attention, but what would that achieve? I'd heard the internal click of the door locks, imprisoning me in my metal cage. So far the evil bastard had covered his bases well. He'd thought this out. Planned well. I'd need to be on extra-high alert for a window of opportunity to escape.

What would Harley do? Shit. Harley! Glancing at the clock on the dash, I figured he'd probably be gearing up to leave the apartment to come pick me up. What would he do when I failed to appear? When staff failed to find me? Would he call Viper? It only consoled me slightly. By then I could be miles away, hurt or…worse.

Even with military resources at their fingertips, time would be their enemy. God. Once we were out of the hospital parking lot, how would they ever find me? I could only hope, because I hadn't been killed yet, that somebody wanted me alive for whatever sick reason they had.

A bargaining chip? That idea suddenly had me stiffen further. My trashed apartment. Harley's shooting. Were they connected to this? It made sense. If that were the case, I definitely had become a pawn. To what extent and for how long, I couldn't be sure. I remained alive for now. That would have to do.

Chapter Seven

Harley

Look into it more? Damn straight they would look into it more. In the meantime, I needed a cell or a hospital phone so I could call Viper. Remembering the card he'd given me earlier in the day, I found it my jeans pocket, relieved to feel the smooth cardboard.

"I want every available person you have scouring this hospital until she's found. Do you understand?"

The nurse cowered slightly at my tone, but I couldn't care about that. She didn't know what my gut screamed at me.

Nodding, she padded away.

"Wait!" I called before she disappeared through the door again. "I need to call a friend to let him know. Can I use a phone?"

"Go back out through those double doors," she meekly said, pointing behind me. "Follow the hallway to the end and turn left. The nurses' station is halfway down. They'll let you make a call."

"Thank you." I didn't wait for her to reply. I took off, anger building with each stride. This reeked of my drama transferring over to Mac. I'd brought this to her. If the cocksucker who'd attempted to kill me and then ransacked her apartment had anything to do with this, I would remove his head from his shoulders.

Viper needed to get here pronto and organize to have the cameras scanned. Her disappearance would show up somewhere. We needed to know just what we were dealing with.

Could I be barking up the wrong tree? Panicking for nothing? No. Every cell in my body screamed that she'd met with foul play. It sickened me, but I had to keep my head on straight. I had to dig deep for the soldier inside to take over and not the man who had feelings for his stunning nurse.

I was on a mission, and perhaps I truly had lost the plot, but where Mac was concerned, I didn't want to take any chances. If she turned up in the next few minutes, all would be well and good, but if my hunch proved correct, each second counted.

Arriving at my destination, I placed both hands on the counter and interrupted the woman working at her computer.

"Excuse me. I've been told I could use your phone to make a call. It's important."

Eying me for a moment, she picked up the handset and offered it to me with a short smile. "Dial nine first and then the number."

Grateful, I nodded at her, pressed nine, and proceeded to dial my friend's number.

He answered on the fourth ring.

"It's me, Harley. We have a problem."

Explaining the situation, he listened quietly until I finished.

Being the cool, calm, and collected warrior he was, he asked, "You sure she's not tied up with a patient?"

"If that were the case, she'd be contactable. Someone would know her whereabouts. Besides, she hasn't been seen since leaving to grab a coffee downstairs."

"How long has it been?"

"I've been waiting nearly an hour, but she hasn't been seen for at least a couple of hours." I know it sounded crazy. How could she vanish? What if she'd been called to another wing of the hospital? It did happen, right? That way, the people in her department wouldn't have seen her. But surely she'd have to let someone know. Everything in me screamed *trouble*. Better to overreact than ignore my gut instinct.

"Call whoever can authorize us visual on the security cameras," I ordered, my voice surprising me with its calm yet commanding tone.

Viper replied with a curt, "On it. See you soon."

He hung up, leaving me with the desperate hope that we'd find something on the video footage.

I couldn't lose her. Not happening. Not on my watch. Not after...shit.

Raking both hands across my scalp, briefly pulling on my hair, I found my way back to ICU to await further information. I doubted they'd find any. Hospitals always ran on skeleton staff. As if there would be even one person to spare to search every square inch of the place.

No. Answers wouldn't be found until Viper arrived. I'd just have to sit tight and simmer down. Easier said than done. Steeling myself against the vivid images of the night before and how Mac had surrendered herself to me, I squeezed the edges of the chair tightly, tamping down my heart's attempt at knocking down the emotionless wall I fought to keep erected.

A quick vision of her suffering already at the hands of evil had me standing and pacing.

The deserted waiting room allowed me the space to stride out my frustration. Viper had better bring the God-damned cavalry with him because we'd need all the help we could get.

Seek and destroy. I remember hearing that mantra in my dream-self's head before walking in on Reno strapped to a chair. Fat lot of good that did. I wouldn't let it happen again.

Shoot and ask questions later. Kill or be killed. No hesitation. Each second that ticked by without any trace of Mac felt like a countdown to doom. My instincts were on fire, every cell on high alert.

Each time the ICU door opened, my heart leapt with hope that a stunning blonde would walk through, gifting me with her killer smile. Each time she didn't, I knew my fear had been well-founded.

It seemed forever before I turned and spotted my friend striding toward me.

"Hey man. I got here as quick as I could." A slap on the back failed to appease my jittery nerves.

"Jesus, man. I need some asshole's heart ripped from their chest," I growled. "What have you got for me?"

"Hospital security is sending through footage as we speak. Do you think it's related to Reno's captor? He was the leader of the cell we brought down. That has to have some kickback."

Letting all the air out of my lungs in a rush, I conceded, "It's looking more and more like it. If that's the case, Mac is in deep shit. Fuck, Viper. How the hell do we deal with this?"

Before he could respond, his cell pealed out into the quiet.

"Viper."

I listened for any sign of what was being said on the end of the line, but with my friend's one word answers it proved difficult.

The call ended and he pinned me with a hard look.

"Sit down."

"Bullshit I will. Tell me. Where is Mac?"

Rage singed my insides. I could tell this wouldn't be good. My teeth clenched together, my jaw a rigid plane of knotted muscle. A pivotal moment where everything would change.

Staring at Viper's face for any sign of distress proved futile. He had wiped all emotion away and stood rigid—almost inhuman. Pity I couldn't hold the same composure. My face scrunched up, eyes squinting as he began.

"A male of Eastern appearance, dressed in doctor's scrubs entered an elevator with her. They both exited at the basement and got in a black SUV. My guy's running the plates now."

I almost collapsed as my legs threatened to give

out. Catching my balance, I skulked to the wall of the small waiting room and pounded my fist into it. Once. Twice. Three times.

A hand on my shoulder and a forceful pull backward stopped me from punching it a fourth time.

"I know you're raging right now, man, but we need to focus. Save your anger for the dead man walking."

Damn straight. The hunter just became the hunted. So help me, I couldn't wait to give him a slow, painful death.

Chapter Eight

Mac

The sun dimmed and so did my hope. We'd been traveling nearly an hour. Inside his black SUV was another man of Middle Eastern appearance whom I hadn't noticed until we were out onto the main road. He also had a gun aimed at me.

I hadn't spoken and neither had my captors. With each minute that ticked by, I became more anxious. Being locked in a vehicle on the move to God knows where didn't bode well for me. By the time anyone realized I'd vanished from the hospital I would probably be too far gone to be found. Blood surged in my ears at the hopelessness of the situation. I should have raised the alarm before getting locked in the car. Would the gunman really have opened fire on innocent staff and patients? And more to the point, should I have called his bluff? Ugh. Too late now.

When Harley arrived to pick me up, I wouldn't be there. What would he do? I had a fair idea, but how in the hell would I ever be found? How much time did I have left before they killed me? Although, if they wanted me dead, why bind my hands and drive me anywhere? They'd obviously been watching me for a while.

I sank back into the seat, watching the sign for Detroit appear. Ugh. Really? With a population of over 670,000, it would be easy for us to disappear. Maybe the plan entailed that. Why though? I had a million questions running through my brain, and the more I thought about it, the more I wondered if they would use me as leverage to draw Harley out.

Exhaustion began to set in, but I couldn't allow myself the luxury of falling asleep. I needed all my faculties. I needed to wait for my captors to let their guards down. While not wanting to risk my safety further, staying focused might be my only chance.

Finally, the vehicle jerked left as we crawled through the city center to a rough part of town, turning into an underground parking garage beneath an unassuming two story building wedged between a laundromat and a vacant, boarded-up shop.

Winding down his window, the driver spoke in a foreign accent into an intercom. A second later the large security door barring anyone access lifted, allowing us entry.

My hands shuddered and a gag erupted from my throat as bile swirled up my esophagus in despair. My throat burned. While we'd been on the road and moving, I'd been relatively safe. And alive. Now, I couldn't be one hundred percent sure. Even being used as leverage, they could do whatever they pleased to me. I just wanted to wake up from this nightmare and be back in the staff cafeteria at the hospital, awaiting a coffee.

If this had anything to do with Harley, why take me? Why not target him alone as they had when he'd been shot? They obviously wanted him dead, and had ample opportunity to take him out. What game were they playing? They didn't need me as a bargaining chip.

Remembering my cell sat in the leg pocket of my scrubs, I prayed they wouldn't search me and confiscate it. If given the opportunity, I could send an SOS to Viper. Thank God, I had his number in my address book.

Drawing his gun out again and aiming it at me again as we parked in the almost vacant lot, the driver spat, "Get out!"

Staring down the barrel of metal, a stabbing pain quickly shot through my chest. He could pull the trigger at any moment if he chose to and I'd lose everything. My breathing had practically stopped in fear. Now that we had arrived at our destination, the reality of the situation gripped me hard. I froze.

And then the unthinkable happened. My cell vibrated to alert me of an incoming call. Shit. Shit. The twisted eyes of the goon next to me widened in manic anger, and before I knew what was happening, he had the gun pressed to my temple and screamed, "Give me your cell! Now!"

The dig of metal had me whimpering as my fingers fumbled into my pants to retrieve my cell. Before I handed it to him, I momentarily glanced at the screen.

Char.

Snatching it out of my hand, he opened his door and threw it as far as he could. I watched in horror as it smashed on the concrete, my lifeline gone.

Turning back, he barked at me in his native tongue, and while I couldn't understand the words, the venom with which he spoke drove a line of terror up my spine.

Without warning, he flicked his hand and drove the butt of the gun into my head, hard, jarring me to the right. Pain sizzled through my scalp and my hands instinctively came up to cradle the point of impact. He still screamed, but changed his lingo to English at the last moment.

"Get out! Get out!"

My head throbbed. Both men exited and hovered, waiting for me to follow them. When I faltered through sheer terror, one man leaned in and ripped the seatbelt off before dragging me from the car. It all happened so fast, I couldn't think. Both men spoke to each other in a foreign tongue.

Tears began falling from the blow I'd taken, and the very real dread of being led to my death. I'd had no time to say goodbye to anyone. My parents were happily vacationing. Living life to the fullest without a care in the world. If I died, their world would come crashing down.

I stumbled, unable to walk in a straight line with the way both men pushed me along, my shattered cell crunching under my flats as I attempted to keep up.

My body and mind were disjointed. Not working together. My brain tried to come up with a plan, but couldn't, because at the same time, it registered the pain of my attack and had a hard time focusing on anything other than the agony in the side of my head.

We approached an elevator and hustled inside when the door opened. The building didn't look tall enough to have one, but what did I know? It flicked through my brain in a millisecond and I internally laughed at my stupid observation in such a desperate time. Perhaps my mind had shifted into survival mode to protect me against a total meltdown.

In another few seconds we were exiting into a large warehouse-type room. Two other similar-looking men stopped what they were doing to watch us. Four against one.

My captors threw me into the middle of the space and began raving like lunatics, waving their arms around as they rattled off in their own language. The other two closed toward me, causing me to stiffen and then cower. Insufferable odds.

My earlier tears had stopped momentarily but flowed freely again as I watched and waited.

Four hate-filled faces surrounded me as I spun each time they inched closer.

"Please!" I begged. "Don't hurt me." No more than the first asshole already had with his gun.

The tallest guy wearing scruffy jeans and a black shirt laughed at my futile plea. He crept forward until he stood before me. His eyes bored into me, dark as night. Evil as sin. He lifted a hand and I flinched, expecting him to harm me, but instead he held my chin steady. With an unconvincing grin, he spoke.

"So. You are our lure, hmm?" Moving my chin from side to side, he studied me, his eyes dropping to my nurse's scrubs, the stupid smile plastered in place. I wanted nothing more than to wipe it off with my fist, but it would only get me killed sooner. I needed to remain compliant for now. To assess my situation and figure out why they were using me as a bargaining chip.

The word 'leverage' played over and over on repeat in my mind. It definitely had something to do with Harley. Did that mean they wanted to trade me for him?

I couldn't do it. He'd been through too much already. I couldn't feed him to the wolves. If I had to sacrifice myself, then so be it. I would. Even though I didn't want to die, I'd had a good life thus far, apart from Nick and I, but that seemed small fry compared to the battles Harley had been involved in. I'd saved many lives in my career. My own existence hadn't been in vain.

Staring my would-be killer down, I steeled my spine, determined that if my fate already involved death, then I wouldn't go down cowering.

For a brief second, his eyes flickered at my change in demeanor, and then he licked his lips as if my slight show of courage turned him on in a sick way.

Repulsed by his hands on me, I pulled back but didn't get very far. A fierce slap to my face made me cry out, as the force of it threw my head to the right. My neck jarred, bringing about sharp shooting pain at the base of my skull. I needed to simmer down and comply, but that proved easier said than done when everything in me screamed to fight for my life.

The guy who had gripped my chin and slapped me apparently didn't like my resistance regardless of his continued smirk. He towed me as if I were nothing but a bag of garbage to a wooden chair sitting against a large, dirty window. He threw me down and barked at one of his goons, who disappeared and returned with rope.

In a moment he'd tethered me to the chair, my torso bound. He failed to be gentle, as the restraint bit into my chest.

"Please. I won't say anything. Let me go and I'll forget this happened." I knew I clutched at straws and that they had no intention of freeing me until they got what they wanted. Namely Harley, or should I now call him Declan?

Had I known he would come with such danger, I wouldn't have taken him into my home. Perhaps doing the right thing had ended up being my downfall.

I wished I were at my apartment reading or doing something mundane like loading the dishwasher or toiling with the laundry. I'd willingly go back to my boring life in a heartbeat if it would put me out of harm's way.

Every sound and smell came to life, as if my mind prompted me to take in the tiniest of details, either due to the flight or fight response, or whether to assist police when it came time for my rescue. *My rescue.* That seemed the most unlikely of scenarios at present. I may be able to recall how dank the warehouse smelled or how the skitters of rats or mice sounded behind me occasionally, or descriptions of my captors, but all of that information wouldn't actually help me get freed. I didn't have a hand in that at all.

I searched the large space looking for an out. The only other door apart from the one I had come through stood on the far right wall. A bathroom perhaps? If I said I needed to pee, could I lock the door and climb through a window? Doubtful. Why would they make it easy for me?

Still, it could be my only lifeline. I needed to get untied.

"I need to use the bathroom." Shooting all of the men a pleading look, I waited for their reply.

They simply laughed at me. Each of them. While I wasn't desperate, I could feel pressure on my bladder. I'd been going to use the bathroom at the hospital on my break but had never made it.

Sagging my shoulders, most of the fight left me. Glancing at my watch, I noted the time was seven p.m.

Harley would be frantic. So would Char after attempting to call me earlier and failing. I took little comfort in the fact that the authorities had probably been notified. The waiting game had my name on it.

Chapter Nine

Harley

A nurse I recognized from my stay in the hospital exited a door and made her way over to us.

Concern marred her features.

"Hi Harley, I'm Charlotte. I'm not sure if you remember me from your time here. I'm a friend of Mac's. What's going on? I tried calling her cell numerous times but it remains unanswered. I've tried again and again but can't get through. She never returned back to work. Where is she?"

I could tell she was attempting to remain strong, but tears swelled at the corner of her eyes. She looked between me and Viper.

Sighing out a weighty breath, I wasn't sure how much to tell her. Chancing a glance at Viper, he nodded for me to speak.

"We have reason to believe she met with foul play. Cameras show her leaving with a male and getting in to a black SUV."

"Jesus! Have you called the police? Are they

looking for her? What are you still doing here? Shouldn't you be doing something?"

Her face became frantic. I could feel Viper tense beside me at the woman's impending breakdown.

"We've got men on it. We were just about to leave when you came out," I appeased her.

"I'm coming with you. I want to help look for her."

"What?" I asked, stunned. No way.

"I've finished work now. I'm coming. If I have to I'll damn well go and look for her myself."

Viper finally said, "Bullshit, you will. You need to go home, Ma'am, and sit tight. We'll handle it."

Resting her emotional stare on my friend, she shook her head. "Like hell! Mac is my friend. I've known her a long time. I want to help."

Placing both hands on her hips in a show of defiance, I couldn't help but admire the will of the stubborn woman. She clearly loved Mac. I couldn't blame her for wanting to help."

Turning back to Viper, I said, "It won't hurt. We don't know Mac as well as Charlotte. Maybe she can give us vital information."

Gripping my arm and leading me away from the anxious woman, Viper whispered in a low voice, "You can't be fucking serious, man! This is heavy shit. I won't bring an innocent female into it. There's already one been taken. We don't need any more."

Knowing he had a valid point but not wanting the woman to go off half-cocked on her own, I made a suggestion. "If she wants to come with us, she can follow us to your place and wait there. That way we can keep an eye on her until we figure out our course of action. We can't exactly just go driving around aimlessly searching for an SUV that is probably out of town by now. As much as it burns my blood, we need to wait for intel."

Giving me a death stare, he nodded curtly. "Fine, but she's your responsibility."

Heading back to Charlotte, I filled her in on our plan. She still didn't look happy but agreed to follow us to Viper's place.

***

Darkness closed in. We'd arrived at Viper's house a little over an hour ago. I felt the dread building with each second that passed.

Viper's cell pealed out, making both Charlotte and I jump. We sat on the couch with an enlarged map of the city spread out before us waiting on city surveillance to track the vehicle and get back to us.

"Go." My friend had a cell reserved for military calls so he dismissed formalities.

"Aha. Yep. Can we get a couple of men to check it out? Good. Get back to me with details."

The call ended.

"What did they say?" I asked, standing from the sofa, ready to leave if needed. It had been pointless going on a search of the city. We had nothing to go on yet.

"Vehicle is registered to Mohammad Ahmed. He's leasing an apartment in the city. Two men are on their way over to search for clues. He has links to the cell leader we killed. I'd bet my life he shot you and trashed Mac's apartment. He won't be working alone."

My hands clenched so hard my fingers hurt. "She's in grave danger, man. Sitting here, I feel so helpless. It's driving me insane."

Nodding in understanding, Viper pocketed his cell. "As soon as we hear from our surveillance guy, we'll have a clue as to whether they left the city and the direction they headed."

"It's taking too long," I snarled.

"Damn straight it's taking too long. I would have been out searching by now, but 'His Highness' over there won't let me go look." Charlotte piped up.

Viper had banned her from going off on her own in the hunt for her friend. So far she'd merely been sitting on the couch, frustrated, and I couldn't blame her. I hated waiting. There must be something we could do.

Viper stalked toward her. "And where are you going to look, huh? Do you have any idea? Do you think she's going to magically appear out of thin air? You have no idea who we're dealing with here. Like I said at the hospital, I suggest you go home and wait for us to call."

Rather than cower down to him, because in all honesty he looked pretty scary in a macho, pretty boy kind of way, she stood her ground and lifted her face defiantly. Yep, she had balls.

"Excuse me! You can't boss me around or keep me from doing anything! In fact, I'm leaving. At least driving around, I feel like I'm actually doing something. She could be dead by now…"

Her voice trailed off as she hurriedly moved to

the front door, retrieving her purse from the small table beside it. I truly did feel for her and I knew her anger came from a place of love for Mac. I hated seeing her leave like this.

"Charlotte, wait!" I called out.

She turned slowly, her eyes glassy. I agreed with Viper about her not getting involved, so I said the only thing I could. "We'll call you as soon as we find out anything. I know you feel as helpless as I do right now, but Viper has more resources at his fingertips than the local police. You have to trust him to find her." It sounded hollow as I said it, but we needed to remain positive.

Her mouth pressed into a quivering line and her eyes softened, but she didn't add anything and quietly let herself out.

Guilt swamped me. Turning to my friend, I blurted out, "Did you have to be such a dick to her about it?"

Viper had both hands clasped behind his neck, glaring at the ceiling as if at war within himself. He stood like a marble monolith, every bit the warrior, arms almost busting the seams of his shirt.

"She needed to be told the cold, hard truth. I won't put anyone else at risk. If she goes off half-cocked, she's going to endanger herself. I can't be looking out for her and helping you find Mac."

He had a very good argument. Hopefully Charlotte would just drive around town for a bit and then return home.

Viper's cell rang again. He gave me a brief scowl before turning on his heels and walking into the kitchen. The sound of his voice quieted as he moved away.

My heart thudded double time, bringing about an ache in my chest where my wound sat. Perching on the edge of the sofa, unable to relax, I awaited the intel that would hopefully bring us a step closer to finding the woman who had burrowed under my skin, big time. I didn't know what I'd do if anything happened to her. She'd been my constant since I'd awoken from my coma. My memory could remain locked away forever as long as she came back to me. Realizing the depth of my feelings, one thing became clear. I had fallen for my kind-hearted, stunning nurse. Clarity washed over me. Unsure what she felt in return, it didn't matter at this point. I would kill for her. I would stop at nothing to bring her home. She'd spent her life caring for others and now she needed someone to fight for her. Unlike her ex-boyfriend, Nick, I would be that person. I didn't need convincing.

Viper strolled back in with two beers in his hand. He threw one at me and I caught it midair.

Perhaps some alcohol would quell my disquiet. Doubtful but worth a try.

"So, the CCTV shows the vehicle driving through town and leaving on Interstate 94. My guess is Detroit's the destination. There's nothing much in between. I can't imagine suspected terrorist members holing up in some hick town in the middle of nowhere. It doesn't make sense. I'm going to get some men from the area to scour the city and any cameras that may be able to pick up the vehicle. Sarge is getting a team together as we speak." Pocketing his phone, he added, "Tomorrow we need to get you a cell."

I blew out a deep breath. At least we had some sort of a lead and backup. Hopefully Viper's call about Detroit would prove correct, otherwise we'd be wasting everyone's time. I hoped Mac remained safe until we found her. From what little memory I had in combat, those assholes were ruthless and didn't care about casualties.

"So what now?" I popped the top off my beer and took a long swig, letting the cold soothe some of the burn.

Plopping down on a chair, Viper shut his eyes. "Now we wait."

Chapter Ten

Mac

All the men except one left, which pleased me. They had ogled me like a fresh piece of meat. Now that I'd been captured and restrained, their part in the sick plot had ended.

The ringleader skulked toward me, his satanic eyes fixed on me. I shivered as he stopped within touching distance.

His hand stretched out and his knuckles grazed the length of my neck. "You and I are going to get to know each other better."

Turning my face away from him, not wanting to witness the depraved thoughts written all over his face, my rebuttal didn't last long. Another hard slap had me sitting front and center again, my eyes finding his black polo shirt. Still, I couldn't look at him. How did one stare down evil and not lose it? I needed to keep it together. I didn't want to give him my fear. He had everything else.

The sting rose in my cheek and lanced outward

into my temple and down my jaw. A short, sharp whimper escaped but I didn't allow any more.

"Do not cower away from me!" he roared, seizing my chin and thrusting my face upward so that I had no choice but to focus on him. "Now. Let me introduce myself. My name is Mohammad Ahmed. Your friend killed one of my top men, and now I come seeking revenge."

My insides plummeted, my worst fears being confirmed. This man had shot Harley. It had all been connected to his life in the military. Reno. His nightmare.

Not waiting on a reaction from me, he continued, his grip on my jaw increasing.

"Here's what's going to happen. I'm going to use you as bait to draw him out. He has feelings for you, yes?"

My eyes expanded fully, my predicament and earlier suspicions becoming crystal clear. My life for Harley's. My abduction had sealed his fate. Why though? Why do it this way?

"Why didn't you just take another shot at him when you found out he had survived the first attempt on his life?"

They could have ended his life the day we spent at the festival in town. There had been plenty of opportunity.

"That's too easy. We now have leverage. This way, he'll not only suffer because we have you, he'll suffer when we get him. He'll wish for death when we're finished with him."

I gagged. I hoped to God Harley would bring the entire military with him because he'd need it. If only my phone hadn't been destroyed, perhaps I could have dialed Viper's number inconspicuously and had a trace done on my location.

My life essentially sat in Harley's hands and his in mine, bizarre as that sounded. God. The 'more' I'd craved in my mundane existence hadn't encompassed this.

Never in a million years did I ever imagine I'd be caught up in a military war with my hot patient as one of the key players.

I kidded no one. He'd stopped being my patient the moment I allowed him into my home. The moment I wanted him to kiss me. Perhaps even the moment he'd opened his eyes and stolen my breath.

Would I swap those exciting, heated moments and all that went with them? To never have experienced the rush of pure hormonal adrenalin? No. If I died during my attempted rescue at least I'd felt alive for a short amount of time. Quality, not quantity. Right?

Jerking upright, my mind focused on the present and the hand that had worked its way from my jaw down to my breast. Oh no. Not happening.

Snarling in an attempt to redeem some of my power, I ground out, "Don't touch me. Keep me here as long as you want, but don't touch me!"

I knew before I'd finished it would come with consequences, and sure enough, he lowered himself so his face shadowed mine, gripping my breast so hard my teeth clenched and my eyes squeezed tight. His other hand came to my head, where he fisted a handful of my hair and pulled hard.

"Shut up! You are in no position to make

demands!" With that he licked a trail up my jaw and began sucking on my ear, all the while pain stabbed into me where his hand remained squeezing my breast. My skin squirmed upon his touch.

The nightmare had just begun.

Chapter Eleven

Harley

"Pack a bag, some cash, and weaponry. We're heading to Detroit." Viper stalked through to his bedroom, leaving me with the rest of my beer and some carnal instinct that roared to life inside me at the thought of driving into danger. My blood sang and every sense came to life like I'd been born to battle.

Downing the remains of the beer, I made my way to the spare room to pack. Finally. We were doing something. I'd be closer to her. Closer to getting her back. I'd never let her go again. I wanted her in my home. My bed. And most importantly in my life. Permanently. Nothing would come between us again. She put me back together. Brought me to life. What I lacked, she made up for. Yin and yang. Her softness complemented my hardness. Her radiance shone on my darkness.

She's the air I needed to breathe. If, no when, I got the chance, I'd tell her how I felt.

We were packed and on the road in less than half an hour. Night driving would give us a clear run. Viper had booked a hotel in the center of town for an undisclosed amount of time. I'd already made the decision that if it came down to it, I'd trade myself for her. No hesitation. She could go back to doing what she did best…saving lives. She mattered to so many. I'd die happily knowing her life would return to normal, even though I wouldn't be a part of it.

Viper need not know. He'd rage at me for even contemplating it after losing Reno, but I'd be damned if I'd watch someone else close to me die. Because of me.

"You holding up okay?"

Glancing sideways, I watched the passing shadows dance and disappear across his face with the street lights. He'd switched into full-on soldier mode, I could tell. His eyes had a detached look to them. I wish I could do the same, but this mission wasn't some assignment we'd been given. This planned rescue held my heart in its hands and it squeezed tighter with each passing second.

Staring back out the window, a vision caught me off guard and quickly transported me out of Viper's car and somewhere far, far away.

Digesting what I'd just been told by my best friend, anger breached every molecule in my heart and soul. I'd been torn into shreds. How had I not seen the signs? How could she do this to me? How could he?

Listening to her car pull into the driveway, I

waited. Heeled footsteps played a staccato on the concrete path leading to the front door. My truck took up extra room in the garage so she always parked outside.

The door opened. Her business attire, including a skin-tight skirt failed to pull any emotion other than rage from me.

"Dec. Hey!" She beamed as she shut the door and strode over to me, pausing halfway after scanning my face.

"Honey? Are you okay? What's wrong?" She knew better than to move forward.

"What's wrong? You know damn well what's wrong! How long? Huh? How long has it been going on?"

Confusion marred her perfect features before recognition set in. Lines cut into her forehead and her face paled. My fingers were coiled into my palms, every muscle in my arms constricted.

"Dec. Let me explain."

I cut her off with my palm facing out. "Don't bother. Viper told me everything. While I've been off earning money, keeping my family and this country safe, you've been getting it on with one of my best friends. I'd say that explains it perfectly."

Tears ballooned and tumbled down her cheeks. She shook her head as if denying my accusations.

"It...I...you were gone so much. I didn't mean for it to happen." What more could she say?

I took a step forward, needing to hit something but knowing it would never be her or any woman. My chest cracked wide open as I looked at the woman I loved. The woman who had promised to love me till death do us part. To honor.

"How long?" I could barely get the words out. They sounded more like a snarl.

"Six months." She swiped at her wet cheeks. Normally her tears would call me to kiss them dry, but tonight, I welcomed her remorse. I needed her tears.

"You screwed Reno for six months?"

"No. I mean, yes."

I roared to the ceiling. I'd watched Reno take his last breath two months ago. It had taken Viper that long to tell me about the affair. It all made sense now. Reno's last apology. "I'm sorry, man." He'd been talking about his affair with my wife. If he hadn't been killed in battle I would have beaten the shit out of him.

"So let me get this straight. You fucked my friend. I attempted to save his life while watching him slip away. I grieved for him. I'm still grieving. And this whole time you've carried your little secret, pretending to be the supportive wife, comforting me when I lost it? Holding me when I needed you to? What? Are you glad he died so you could escape getting found out?"

My head exploded. My thoughts scattered.

"No! It wasn't like that. I grieved too!"

"I bet. If Viper hadn't told me, you would have carried it to your grave."

"I wanted to tell you. So many times. But you suffered when you came back from battle. Your demons changed you. The nightmares and mood swings. I just didn't want to add to that."

"Spare me the favors, okay?" I screamed.

She shrank away and took a step back.

"I loved you. I fucking loved you and you made a mockery of it!"

"Please!" she begged. "We can get through this. I don't want to lose you."

Laughing, I choked out, "You lost me when you took your clothes off for someone I trusted with my life."

Unable to stay in the same room with her, I called over my shoulder, "I want you and all your stuff gone when I get back. Leave the key on the table and lock the door on your way out."

She cried out, "I'm sorry!" as I slammed the door.

I was startled by Viper shaking me. My reality changed back to the passenger seat inside a car. He was in my face. "Hey. Man. Snap out of it! It's me. You're okay!"

What the hell? My eyes focused on my worried friend.

"Where were you? You spaced out on me!"

We'd pulled over onto the road shoulder.

"I remember."

"You remember? All of it?"

"No. I remember the moment I confronted Trudy about her affair with Reno. You confessed everything to me."

Falling back into his seat, he exhaled long and loud. "I'm sorry, bro. That's twice I've had to do that to you. The second time proved no easier."

"I'm glad you did. I needed to know who I married. If Reno hadn't died, they'd probably still be screwing each other."

"Let it go, man. It's in the past. I know it seems like it's still fresh because of your memory loss, but you got over it. You got over *her*."

"She told me we were in the process of getting back together."

"Lies. All lies," he snapped.

"You didn't like Trudy, did you?"

"Something about her rubbed me the wrong way." He eased the car forward again.

Obviously I'd been too blind to see it. Too in love. Too trusting.

Mac wouldn't do that to me. Trudy and she were nothing alike.

"Maybe I should trust your instincts," I offered Viper.

"You always did."

Arriving on the fringes of Detroit, a shiver wrapped around me. Forewarning? I couldn't be sure, but I knew one thing. I *felt* Mac. Some weird sensory thing I'd woken up with. Viper had been correct in his assumption about coming here. I needed to reassure myself he'd get her out alive.

His cell rang, so we swerved to the curb so he could answer it.

"Intel?" he offered curtly. "Yep. Roger that."

He disconnected and hit the gas. "One of the CCTV cameras picked up the vehicle a few hours ago driving past the Institute of Arts Museum. They've still got to get their hands on more footage throughout the city that may be available. It's a start."

Thank God. It appeared we were taking small

baby steps, but at least we were moving forward. I needed to know Mac wasn't hurt. Everything could change in a second.

The dash clock read twelve a.m.

We'd do a drive around before hitting the hotel. See if we could figure out any likely places some radical extremists might take a hostage. Or maybe by some miracle, spot something suspicious.

I'd stashed five thousand dollars cash in the false bottom of my duffel bag for living expenses and emergencies. Viper had some money too, so we were set financially. I didn't want to be in Detroit any longer than a few days, because each day that passed lowered Mac's chances of survival.

There were still plenty of people out and about driving as we continued along Michigan Avenue.

It would be easier to spot potential trouble or threats once we turned off the main road into town and scoured the side streets. Fingers crossed we'd get a more direct location of the vehicle before the night ended. We had to. I'd be a mess by morning. I could feel myself only just holding together by a frayed thread that could break at any moment.

I didn't know what we expected to find by driving past the Arts Museum, but we did it anyway before turning off and weaving our way around the maze of downtown.

"Hungry?" asked Viper.

"You want food?" How could he eat? My gut felt like someone fisted it. Then again, Viper didn't have his woman's life at stake. "Nah, man. I'm good. I could use a coffee though. I need to remain vigilant."

"You're gonna need sleep, you know that, right?"

Sleep wouldn't be happening until we found Mac. Coffee would be my savior until then.

"Not happening." I looked sideways for him to push it further but he kept quiet with just a nod of his head.

"I guess at this time of night, McDonalds coffee it is."

"You come to Detroit often?" I still didn't remember much about my best friend. He appeared to know his way around the city.

"I've been here enough times to know where I'm going." He smiled at me and swerved to miss a pedestrian.

"All right then. McDonalds it is."

Quite frankly I didn't care where I got caffeine from, as long as it wired me.

My eyes scoped as many of the streets as possible, but to no avail.

With a double-shot tall black, my fatigue waned, allowing me to focus. Viper had been quiet the whole time, hopefully because he'd been concentrating.

"You get anything?" I asked.

"No. I think we're wasting our time. Let's head to the hotel and wait."

The idea of being cooped up within four walls already had claustrophobia clawing at me. Waiting meant we weren't doing. Doing meant we were at least attempting to find Mac.

What I'd give to have her in my arms right now. I'd forego my memories forever if she could be here sitting beside me. Safe.

She shouldn't have gone to work. We should have taken her to a safe house. The break-in at her apartment had been a warning we should have heeded. But hindsight only proved to be a bitch. She had gone to work. She had been abducted. Now we had to deal with it.

"Fine," I ground out. My rigid jaw ached from gnashing my teeth together. And my neck and shoulders had stiffened to the point of pain.

Once we'd checked in and unloaded our bags, money, and weaponry, Viper made a call to get an update while I took a hot shower to try and loosen my tense muscles.

The cutting spray merely stung instead of relaxing me, so I washed myself, including my hair, and got out to see if anything new had developed.

Viper handed me his cell as soon as I appeared in the living room of the two bedroom suite.

My brows lifted in question, but he didn't reply, so I took the phone. "Hello?"

"Dec?"

Trudy. Tired of correcting her, I answered with a simple, "Yeah."

"Where are you? What's going on?" She sounded frantic, although I couldn't understand why, considering what I'd learned about her affair with Reno.

"I'm...uh...on an assignment." I didn't want to let her know Mac had been kidnapped. "Why do you ask?"

"I've been to your apartment, Viper's, and Mac's. There's nowhere else you would have gone, so I got worried. For a moment, I thought…"

She trailed off, knowing I'd been a target for a homicide.

I felt like being an asshole to her as the gravity of everything cut the ragged cord my nerves hung by. "You thought what, Trudy? You thought you'd come and apologize about the affair you had with Reno that I recently found out about for the second time, and everything would go back to being normal? What did you actually think?"

Viper's smirk widened at my tone. He already disliked my ex-wife, so I imagine he reveled in my curtness.

A gasp on the other end of the line stamped some satisfaction on my heart. "Dec. I'm so sorry. I didn't mean for it to happen."

"Nah. Cheaters never do. You lied to me. And not only about that. You told me we'd been trying to work things out!" My voice rose as anger, heated my blood.

"I've never stopped loving you. We were married. We took vows. Till death do us part. I wanted to try and get back what we had."

"Woman, you're delusional if you ever thought that would happen. As much as I don't recall what happened, I'm telling you now. It's over. I don't feel anything for you. Pity maybe." I wanted to hang the fuck up on her. Quiet sobs echoed through the phone.

"Listen, I'm busy. I gotta go…"

"Wait! I didn't call to discuss our relationship. I called to let you know your mom contacted me, asking about you."

Christ. I'd forgotten all about my mother in light of the situation at hand. I'd planned on paying her a visit, but that would have to wait now. Should I call her? Perhaps that would be the best alternative until I could take Mac with me for support. Not tonight though.

"What did you tell her?"

"I told her you'd only just got back from your mission and you'd be in touch shortly."

Changing the cell to my other ear, I nodded at Viper as he handed me a glass of whiskey, knowing what I needed. Taking it, I downed a long swig before replying.

At least she hadn't mentioned my shooting. "Thank you. I'm glad you didn't mention anything about me almost dying. As much as I don't remember her, I could only imagine what she would go through if she knew." I wasn't a total robot. I still had emotions that were fully functional. While I had lost all respect for the woman on the other end of the line, I was happy she'd used her head.

"So when are you coming home?" she asked.

"Home?"

"Back to Ann Arbor."

I didn't care for her asking me that. She didn't get to show me she cared at all after screwing my friend. I'd have it out with her at a later date. Not tonight. Jesus. I had more important things to think about. "Not sure. When this assignment is finished. Needing to end the call, I abruptly offered, "I've gotta go. Don't call me. I'll call you."

I didn't wait for her reply, but pressed the 'end call' button and handed Viper his cell.

"What did *she* want?"

"She couldn't get a hold of me to let me know my mother called."

His face softened at the mention of my mother. "You should call her."

Walking to the sofa with my whiskey, I sat heavily, throwing my feet on the coffee table. "I know. I can't deal with that right now until we find Mac. I promise I'll call her. Hell, I'll visit her once we get home."

I heard him sigh out. "She's a good woman and worries about you."

Looking up from my drink, his expression spoke volumes. "You love her, don't you?"

He moved to sit beside me. "She's been like a mom to me since my parents died. You're lucky."

Curious, I asked, "What happened to your parents?"

He glanced away and then back, his jaw set. "Truck hit their vehicle head on."

Shit. "So sorry, man."

He shrugged. "Don't worry about it. For what it's worth, you came to the funeral. They both loved you."

Damn. I'd been so wrapped up in my own life, I hadn't asked questions about Viper's.

"That must be shitty. To lose both at once." Even if I can't remember my Mom, I know she's alive.

My heart went out to him. I should have known such personal information. I shouldn't have been hearing it for the first time. I felt like the worst friend. "Man. I don't know what to say. I can't begin to imagine what you've endured. What frustrates me even more is the fact I have no knowledge of any of it."

"Yeah, well. Sometimes I wish I had no memory of it." He finished his own coffee and set it on the coffee table.

Viper's regular cell pealed out. The one not connected to the military. He shot me a quick look and answered it.

"Hello? No. I said we'd let you know if we found anything. We're waiting on intel. We are doing everything we can to find her." My friend had tensed further at the person on the other end. "Look, I really gotta go. You need to let us do what we do best. We'll call you as soon as we hear anything."

He hung up.

I looked at him questioningly.

Glancing at me, he offered, "Charlotte."

"She's just worried."

"I know, but she better not keep calling me every few hours, I swear." Standing, he asked, "You want a drink from the mini bar?"

"Nah, man, I'm good. Why don't you go get some sleep?"

"Shouldn't you be doing that too?"

"Should, but can't. I'll camp here on the sofa for the night. I want to be ready to leave at a moment's notice."

He clapped me on the back. "Good to have you back, man. Even if you're not totally back."

Raising my eyes to his height, I smiled. "It's good to be here and even if I don't know much, I do know you've always had my back."

"Amen, brother. That'll never change."

Obviously deciding against alcohol, he turned and strode down the hallway and closed his bedroom door, leaving me alone to wonder just how the hell we were going to rescue Mac from the worst kind of criminals.

Chapter Twelve

Mac

His hands on me were repulsive enough, but when they progressed to ripping my shirt open and raping my breasts, I'd had enough.

Screaming out and thrashing my body from side to side, moving the chair slightly, I fought for whatever dignity remained. If he took from me what wasn't on offer, I would make it hard for him.

"Get off me, asshole!" I let loose with everything I had, spittle pooling at the corners of my mouth. I'd never been so angry or scared. I needed Harley to come barging through the door to save me, but as each second ticked by, the chances slimmed greatly.

Did he even know I'd been taken from Ann Arbor? And what about the search? Had it begun? If so, it would be in the wrong area.

I didn't have time to ponder any more questions when a fist to my jaw snapped me back to Hades. My face jarred, darkness blocking my vision temporarily. When it returned, the manic face of my attacker hovered close. His black, deranged eyes bored into me with hatred like I'd never seen. A hand clamped around my neck, essentially narrowing my airways.

"You bitch! You do as I say! There is no escape. Fight again and you die!"

I didn't doubt it. I danced with the devil. My life may not be worth as much as I thought. Using me to lure Harley may fail, but they'd have a plan B. Without me, they'd find another way.

The thought made me pull my head in. Fighting might be good in theory, but in actuality it would only hasten my death. I'd need to play along and be a good little hostage for now.

Staring into the depths of depravity, I attempted a nod. His grip on my throat loosened, changing my focus to my cheek. It smarted and throbbed, probably already swelling and bruising. The skin under my eye felt puffy.

Harley, where are you? Please! You have to save me. Find a way. I need you. I saved you. Now it's your turn to save me.

I let the prayer hover in the thick air.

My captor let me go and took a step back, never removing his gaze. I memorized every line and angle of his face should I need to describe him, in the event my rescuers came.

Any light outside had long since faded, a dusky bulb casting a weak glow across the large, sparse room.

I really needed to pee, so I tried my luck a second time.

"Bathroom. I need to use the bathroom," I

pleaded, hoping against all odds he'd take pity on me so he didn't have so smell my urine if he denied my request.

Drawing his gun, which had been tucked into the waistband of his pants, he aimed it at my head.

"Try anything stupid and I shoot. Understand?"

I did. Grateful I'd be able to relieve myself, I replied, "Yes." My voice sounded off with the swelling of my face. My teeth hurt too. Maybe he'd loosened some.

Still with the gun trained at my temple, he began to attempt to loosen the ropes with one hand. When that didn't work, he placed the gun on the floor beside the chair. I wondered if I'd be brave enough to take the opportunity when he loosened the bindings of grabbing the gun and shooting him. Would I get another opportunity? Should I be so stupid as to try after my last attempt? Playing the obedient hostage wouldn't get me free.

Aargh. I didn't know what to do.

Feeling the rope around my chest loosen and drop to the floor, instinct told me to remain seated and obey until told otherwise. If there wasn't a gun involved, I'd attempt to escape. I couldn't risk failing at my attempt or I had no doubt he'd shoot me.

"Get up!" he barked.

Rising, my legs groaned as my joints protested. My butt had gone numb and it took me a second to move forward. The gun retrained on my skull, so I grimaced through the pain and let him push me toward the door. A door leading to the outside world.

Except when I stepped out, a long corridor steered us to a set of stairs. Spurred on by a metal barrel, I descended into a dusty foyer, passing my ticket to freedom. The large steel door was windowless.

Turning the corner into a cramped smaller hall, Asshole shoved me through an open doorway which led to a smelly, dank bathroom that looked like it hadn't been used in years.

Still, I would have peed in a bucket if I had to.

Inside the tiny space, I looked into a smeared mirror, swiping my hands across it to try and clear the grime. My face resembled an abused woman, and rightfully so. As suspected, bruising had begun. The right side of my face from my jaw to just below my eye had been affected. Redness with underlying purple proved a stark contrast to the opposite side. My eye had closed marginally. I looked hideous.

Feeling the onslaught of tears, I tore myself away and went about my business, struggling with my scrub bottoms and underwear because of my shaking hands, before flushing and exiting to await my fate.

On our way up the stairs, my handler's cell rang. He waited until we were at the top before pulling it from his pocket and answering it. He spoke in his native tongue while still prodding me toward the chair.

Ending the call, he threw me down and began restraining me again.

Grinning like the maniac I knew him to be, he said, "It seems your boyfriend is on his way."

Chapter Thirteen

Harley

I must have dozed off because the next thing I knew, Viper shook me awake.

"Get up. We're on the move. Intel's given us a location."

A switch flipped and I rose from the couch, transformed into soldier and savior in an instant.

We'd found her. Nothing else mattered.

Racing into my room, I grabbed my weapon, vested up, and stalked into the hallway, adrenalin kicking me into overdrive. By the time I made it back into the living room, Viper had already left. Locking the suite door, I strode to the bank of elevators. Pressing the button for the basement, I let the car take me to my destiny. I searched for Viper's vehicle and found it not too far away, already running. He hadn't wasted any time. Christ, he must sleep lightly, ready to leave at a moment's notice.

Pulling the door shut, I climbed into the

passenger seat and looked to my friend.

He had his mask on, hard and focused. The heater blasted air into the interior, which helped ease the arctic chill.

"Got your vest on?" he asked, easing out the building onto the street.

"Yep."

"Armed?"

"Of course."

"Let's go get your girl."

With a squeal of tires, we were on our way. My jittery leg jiggled up and down, a million scenario's playing out of how the night would go. I tried to stay positive, but I knew what we were up against and a positive outcome would be hard to achieve, but with my ace up my sleeve that I hadn't mentioned to Viper, I prayed at least Mac would come out unscathed.

We didn't have to travel far. Knowing my girl had been so close failed to appease me. Instead, it amped me even more. I'd been dozing while she'd been held hostage in what I could only imagine were less than ideal conditions.

Game on.

Stopping outside a warehouse in the industrial area of town, we took pause and eased down the street a bit before parking and getting out.

"How are we gonna do this? Are we just going to go in guns blazing?" My memory had stolen precise procedure and protocol of the job.

"Hang five. I need to make sure our men are in position."

I wasn't aware the cavalry had already arrived.

The moment brought back a sense of déjà vu and the dream I'd had in the hospital of our rescue mission in Afghanistan. The one where Reno got killed. It seemed all too familiar. Viper and I going in alone with backup if needed.

Unease snaked its way into my heart. "How many men we got?"

"Three," he replied, switching off his cell and pocketing it.

"Only three?" I'd been expecting more, considering who we were up against. One more thought had me asking the question, "How will you make contact with the men on the outside with your cell off?"

He drew the sleeve of his jacket up to reveal what appeared to be a wristwatch. Upon closer inspection I could tell it wasn't. Two buttons sat on the face. One red, one green.

"Red means wait. Green means go. One press of the green button and our guys will enter with force. It's an alarm everyone is fitted out with. It's specifically only used to alert soldiers outside to hold or move. No one except those requiring backup are authorized to press it."

Raising an eyebrow, I couldn't help but be in awe of the technology. "So if one of our men accidentally pressed the green button before we were ready, our cover would be blown and the shit would hit the fan?"

Viper laughed. I didn't see the question as funny, but he obviously did. "Pretty much, but don't worry, we have a code. Press it once and hold for three seconds, followed by four quick depressions."

Of course we had a code. I couldn't imagine anything connected to the military as being so easy.

"So when are we doing this?"

"No time like the present. We'll head around back. Word has it there's a door, enabling us to be a little less conspicuous."

Nodding, we crept around the block to the rear of the building, stopping just shy of the corner that would direct us to our entry point. Unlike our last mission, I let Viper lead while I had his back, scoping the area for company, both our weapons raised. We used our night goggles rather than relying on exterior or interior lighting. It proved easier to spot targets, moving or still, and would give us the advantage against our enemy.

Viper slowly peered around the corner, his head pivoting back in a microsecond. He held up two fingers, indicating two armed men guarding the door. Both our weapons had silencers, so it would be easy to take them out. Although with one of our snipers apparently positioned in a building across the street, it would be even easier for Viper to order the kill. I got the impression my friend didn't like the easy way, so when he then held up four fingers and began counting down, I prepared myself.

At one, a bead of sweat bubbled just above my right eye, and then we were moving. We both let fire, our targets slumping to the ground simultaneously.

Backing against the wall, we waited for retaliation, and when none came, we inched forward.

Creeping up to the door and stepping over the

107

two corpses, Viper gave it a short pull and gave me the go ahead to follow when it opened. I didn't bother taking stock of the dead men. They played a part in Mac's abduction, so they didn't deserve an ounce of my time.

Obviously someone was expecting us. With two men standing watch at the door, I'd guarantee our intel had been compromised. With the change of game, there posed a new threat. We were stepping into a trap. Viper took pause, probably thinking the same as me. We were sitting ducks. Still, we needed to get inside and assess the situation. We couldn't afford to order 'go' just yet, or it would put Mac in jeopardy. Not that she wasn't already.

Darkness cloaked us, so we moved stealthily, letting our goggles guide us. I made sure to close the door with as little noise as possible. My heart rate soared with each step I took, not knowing what we were walking into, but with my sole focus on getting to Mac.

Fingers crossed we would still have a small element of surprise and our approach hadn't been monitored.

The air smelled musty, like the place had been closed up for months, perhaps years. My ears honed in for any sound, but the only noise came from the wind outside, forcing itself against the back door.

A closed door to our left appeared in the narrow hallway. Viper stopped. We needed to assume any door we came across held Mac inside. With his fingers on the handle, I raised my gun over his right shoulder while searching the hall for any incoming threats.

All clear.

We did the four finger countdown again and Viper pushed open the door. My finger was on the trigger ready, but the room held nothing but a few boxes stacked in the corner.

Moving forward, the bottom floor consisted of three more empty rooms, a bathroom, and foyer leading to the front door and a set of wooden stairs. So far the only threat had been the men guarding the door. I began to wonder just how prepared these guys were for our visit.

Walking around the foyer and past the small bathroom, I froze. Something hit me full force, and yet it would probably evade anyone else. Mac's perfume caught my senses. It lingered in one spot, and then disappeared as if never there. My eyes closed for the briefest moment before instinct had me on guard again. Viper stopped and turned to look at me. I motioned with my hand to proceed, so we eased to the bottom of the stairs.

Mac had been here, and hopefully hadn't been moved to another location. Smelling her perfume lifted my spirits and told me she remained alive. That is, if the scent in the air wasn't the remains of her arrival.

Through my goggles, a patch of heat flared at the top of the stairs. Viper saw it too and held his hand up to wait.

If we took a shot, it could cause an adverse chain reaction.

Our men were placed around the perimeter as backup only. Acting now would be suicide.

Viper motioned back down the hallway. I

followed, not knowing what went through his head.

Opening the first door we'd checked, he motioned me inside.

"We need to distract him. To get him down those stairs. Find something to toss that will make noise."

Searching for anything besides the cardboard boxes proved hard in the dark with only thermals as our guide. Stooping low, I let my hands feel for anything metal such as a screw or shard of glass.

"Find anything?" whispered Viper.

"Nah."

"Keep looking."

Scouring through the boxes, Viper claimed, "This might do."

He held up a small bottle with no label. Perfect.

Before leaving, I listened to the plan.

"I'll throw it up the stairs. You flank the other side out of sight. As soon as someone comes down looking for the source of the noise, we shoot, making sure it's not Mac, of course."

"Right." I couldn't get anything else out, being so keyed up. I needed to draw on my subconscious and trust my soldier instincts would come into play. I didn't want to have to turn myself over but if it came to that, I would.

Giving me a thumbs up, we slipped out of the room and advanced to the staircase. I took my position on the opposite side and waited. Viper acted immediately, tossing the bottle high up the steps. A noise broke out above, a foreign tongue barking rapidly, followed by more than one set of footsteps.

Do or die time.

Watching the color appear through my goggles to signify heat, I aimed, ready to take the shot. A sense of all-knowing flowed into me, allowing me to focus only on the task at hand. Viper took the first shot, and I followed with the second as four men descended, random bullets flying left and right. The first guy hit the floor with the second one falling on top of him. The remaining two attempted to retreat back to the first floor but we were on the move, rising like ghosts, taking out both men consecutively, leaving slumped bodies in our wake.

Upon stepping into the large, open expanse of the warehouse, my eyes immediately zeroed in on Mac, tied to a chair. A dim light shone against the far wall, only allowing enough light to make out her form and nothing else. A lone man stood behind her with a gun to her head, stopping me in my tracks.

Viper screamed, "Arms in the air! Now!"

I could hear Mac whimper, the sound lancing through my chest. Tearing my goggles off and dropping them, I needed to see her. Taking a step closer, I heard the click of the safety being released, forcing me to stop.

Noise behind had me check over my shoulder. I prayed our men had busted in. Instead, two scruffy guys in jeans and tees held rifles at Viper and I. Where had they come from? We'd checked and cleared down below, taking out any threats.

Spinning back around, suddenly feeling as if things were spiraling out of control, I found Mac again.

A sliver of light across her cheek showed me half her swollen, bruised face. Rage had me cry out,

"Mac! Fuck! Are you all right?" Stupid question. One wrong move and she'd take a bullet to the head, but I couldn't think of anything else to ask.

A slight nod from her allowed me to exhale.

The asshole holding the gun smiled sinisterly. "I've been waiting for you to show up."

Indeed. He'd used Mac to lure me here. Well, he had me, and I sure as hell wasn't leaving until Mac walked out safely, consequences be damned.

"Let the woman go. You have me. She's not a part of this," I hollered.

"Oh, but she is. She's my bargaining chip. You see, I've been watching you closely. Finding out you survived the first attempt at killing you only drove my hunger to have you suffer even more."

"Why?" I knew why. Everything in me told me this guy had everything to do with our mission to save Reno and the guy I shot.

The dude's smile vanished, replaced by an angry grimace. "Why? You killed my brother, that's why. And now I'm here to kill you."

His English had an Eastern accent wound through it. My theory had been correct. Everything I'd gone through to get to this moment had been caused by this freak. My memory loss. The break-in at Mac's apartment. Her abduction. And the psycho didn't stop to think that none of this would have happened if Reno hadn't been captured and held hostage in the first place.

I couldn't see the fear I knew would be shooting from Mac's eyes, but I knew it would be the same I'd seen in Reno in his final moments alive.

Shooting a quick glance at Viper, who'd

remained silent since ordering the scum bag to drop his weapon, I watched him press the button on his wrist in the sequence he'd described, to finally order an attack. I just hoped to God our men would enter silently, because if any noise sounded, we were all dead.

Seeing my friend's rock-steady hands holding his weapon at head height, I couldn't tell what went through his mind. He showed no fear. This is what he lived for. He stood tall and proud to be an American and would fight patriotically to the end.

His head never moved, solely focused on his target even though he had two at his back. I guessed we waited on our backup. It would be stupid to make a move now. If they didn't hurry up though, I'd make my move.

I could smell Mac's fear now. Her fear not only for herself, but for me and Viper.

None of this should be happening. Not again. Not with Mac. She was good and innocent. I'd die if anything happened to her because of me. The guy might be using her to lure me, but that didn't mean she'd walk away. We both could be dead soon.

An uneasy sensation crawled over my skin. Something felt off. Our backup should have arrived by now. What took so long? Three Black Ops soldiers ordered to go. My cooler façade began to heat up as each second ticked by.

Asshole spoke. "You have a decision to make, soldier. Your life or hers." He pressed the gun harder to Mac's temple. A noise escaped her and I made my decision.

I couldn't risk her life. I wouldn't make the same

mistake I made with Reno. I couldn't wait for our backup. I just hoped to God when they arrived, they could get us all out of this jam.

With a sudden calm, I dropped my weapon and held up both hands in surrender.

"Dec, what the fuck, man? Pick up your weapon. We got this. That's an order!"

Order be damned. He wasn't my commanding officer. He might have taken charge of this mission, but I answered to no one in this instance. The sensation of doom heightened but I knew I'd made the right decision.

"Don't shoot, Viper. Save yourself and Mac." I growled it out, not taking my eyes off the enemy.

Taking a step closer, Mac's fear became visible. She shook her head at me, tears sailing down her bruised face as I let my eyeballs sway to her then back to the guy I wanted to mercilessly kill.

"I'm here. Take me, but let her go," I offered, inching closer.

"Not happening, man. I'm not letting you do this," Viper roared, desperation lacing his low voice.

"I've made the choice. Mac's life for mine. You need to get her out of here and keep her safe. You shoot and you're dead. I won't stand by and watch anyone else I care about die or suffer."

Shuffling closer, I stopped just shy of Mac, giving her my full attention. I tried to show her everything I felt about her and what I sacrificed. I let my emotions surface and with it came the welling of tears. Who would have thought everything would come full circle. My savior now needed saving.

Perhaps this pivotal moment would prove to be my calling. What I had prepared for my whole life. To die a hero. A martyr. We all had sacrifices to make. Some greater than others. Was I prepared to die? Hell no. Who could possibly be? But knowing she'd live and forever be protected by my wingman strengthened me to face my fate.

Seeing her banged up and desperate confirmed my decision of surrendering. She looked a mess, and all I wanted to do was tear the heart from the enemy standing beside her. If his two lackeys weren't in the room, it would be all over. He's be lying in a pool of his own blood.

Silence still loomed outside and my thoughts began racing at a million different scenarios, the main one being, had our guys been found out and killed? That seemed unlikely considering they were the elite. Even some Afghani rebels trained in combat wouldn't get close to killing a Special Ops soldier.

"I mean it, Dec. Don't do this. Please?" Viper's hard voice bordered on begging. I didn't want to put him in this position, but what choice did I have? Someone in this room would die, but it wouldn't be Mac.

Shaking my head, unable to look my friend in the eyes, I focused on Mac. Even as she sat injured, her strength exuded from her. She still had fight left in her, so I knew she would heal and move forward. Everything I ever needed sat before me, pleading me to back off. Her pain became my pain. I took it in, soaking it into my pores, needing it to spur me on. The fact that I'd die for her spoke volumes about how I felt.

"Mac..." I gritted out, not knowing what the hell else to say.

She whimpered, a tear dripping down her cheek to the corner of her mouth.

"Enough!" barked her captor. "Step forward!"

Without waiting for any more rebuttal, I eased to within touching distance of Mac, feeling the terror rolling off her, curling around me. God. Why did things have to end this way? I wanted to tell her how I felt. I wanted her in my life. I wanted *her*. Being so close and unable to touch her destroyed the remainder of my shattered heart.

"Untie her and let her go." I gave my order, needing this to end. Needing to see her safely with Viper.

The nut job before me grinned as if he'd just won the lottery. His devil eyes sparkled. He enjoyed this way too much.

Fixing me with his hateful stare with the gun still trained on Mac's skull, he dug into a back pocket of his jeans and pulled out a knife. Praying to God he'd honor the deal I made, I stood fixed to the spot.

My heart stuttered, not knowing if he intended to kill Mac anyway. Every muscle in me reacted by coiling tight.

He brought the knife to the rope at the back of the chair and proceeded to cut through it, the sharpness allowing the action to be done in a few seconds. Unraveling it, he watched both Viper and me.

Mac's shoulders were the only things to sag

slightly.

"Dec, I'm warning you. You're making a huge mistake."

Perhaps. Perhaps not. Either way, I held the rights to the decision. Viper couldn't sway me.

Mac suddenly spoke for the first time, startling me. I watched on helplessly as she cried out, "No! I won't let you do this, Harley. I can't. This is who I am. I save people. I saved you once and I will do it again." Turning to leer at the militant, she spoke loud and clear. "Do what you want to me, but let Harley go. Use me as revenge for your brother."

What the actual fuck? Hell no! Not happening. Had she lost her Goddamn mind?

Never going to happen, sweetheart. Nice try, but one I will not consider.

Grinding my teeth, I yelled at her, "Do not say another word, Mac. I applaud your attempt at playing the martyr, but there is no fucking way it's happening. Get that gorgeous butt off that chair and walk slowly to Viper. Now!"

Shocked at my tone, she could do nothing but stare at me. Damn stubborn woman. If I had to grab her and walk her to safety with a gun to my own head, I would. I didn't need to though, because the gun at her head lowered before the prick hoisted her up by the arm and threw her across the floor toward Viper. Still, my hatred for him didn't falter. He hadn't done it in kindness. He wanted me. Nothing more.

I breathed out in relief, turning to watch her scramble up. Viper tucked her into his side protectively, and I knew in my heart that he would be the only one who would safeguard her like I could.

With the gun now trained on me, I waited for instructions.

"Move!" ordered the new thorn in my side.

Leveling Mac with my final stare, I attempted to keep it together as she fell apart.

Her heart bled by way of the emotion in her eyes, indicating her true feelings toward me. She felt what I felt. The pull which ran deeper than affection. I'd felt it the moment I'd looked into her stunning eyes. I knew if we weren't in this situation we could have something incredible. But I had no idea how to fix it. Guns were still trained on Viper, and now Mac, and our team had failed to get us out. I'd seen with my own eyes the call for help using the device strapped to my buddy. Had it not gone through? Something didn't add up.

Her cries cemented themselves in my head. Anguish held me in its grip. I wanted more of her. More of us. We'd only just begun. We had so much potential as a couple. These scumbags were taking everything from me.

My anchor who had kept me grounded was being released, and I felt myself floating again. Right where she'd found me. Floating in a mass of nothing.

Slanting my eyes across at the guy who'd always had my back and who still did by protecting Mac, I sympathized with him. Every muscle in his body twisted tightly and his eyes screamed out to me one last time to rethink my absurd decision. It gutted him to be losing his best friend. As if Reno's death hadn't been a burden almost too heavy to bear, mine would sink him completely. I hated what I needed to do. Hated that I needed to cause them so much pain. I needed to get out of here before I did rethink my decision. But that would get us all killed. Better one of us than three.

Walking past the two people I cared most about, catching Mac's devastated face, I watched helplessly as she broke before me, sobbing openly and crying out.

"No! You can't do this for me! I don't want you to." Her hands reached for me and I let my fingers touch hers, embedding their warmth and softness into my psyche. I'd cling on to the sensation until I took my last breath. The very hands that had treasured my body and tended to my wound. A lifetime ago.

Viper's face pinched with despair, and if I wasn't mistaken his eyes misted over. His neck muscles were ready to pop, his grip on the gun a white-knuckled one.

I mouthed, "thank you," to him and let myself be led out of the room.

Chapter Fourteen

Mac

Watching Harley walk to his death killed me. He would die to keep me alive and it totally ruined me. I couldn't possibly live with that. Why would he sacrifice himself? It should have been me. I tried, but it had been pointless when the enemy had wanted Harley all along. I played no part in the game other than luring the prey to his death.

I looked at Viper, and he appeared as crestfallen as me. We shared a look and he nodded slightly, motioning to me with his fingers in a circular fashion.

Confusion must have marred my features. I wasn't privy to secret military code, so I stood rooted to the spot, devastated. The man who had tried to protect me and had come to mean so much would martyr himself on my account. It left my heart open and bleeding. No one had ever done such a thing.

He cared about me. Way more than I knew. God.

I wanted to do something. Anything.

Momentarily forgetting the two gunmen, I spun to face them, but the room only held Viper and I.

The men had already gone, probably to assist in the killing of Harley. Letting out a loud wail, I fell to my knees, ignoring the jarring sensation. The tear in my heart hurt far worse.

"Are you okay?" Viper squatted next to me, laying his weapon down.

"No. They'll kill him. You need to go after them. I'm fine. I'll catch a cab back to Ann Arbor if I have to. Just go!" My voice had taken on a hysterical tone. A few bruises were nothing compared to watching someone I cared about walk away to their death. I couldn't cope with it.

Pulling up his sleeve, he stared at a device on his wrist with confusion. Pressing a green button a couple of times like some sort of code, he looked back up at me.

"What is that?" I asked, suddenly dog-tired.

"Backup. Except it's either faulty or something is seriously wrong." His mouth pinched tightly. "Can you stand up properly?" he asked, giving me his full attention.

Nodding, I rose before Viper stood and held my arm making sure I didn't teeter.

"I promised Dec I'd watch over you. I can't leave until backup arrives," he affirmed, although I could hear the edge to his voice, as if he warred between leaving or staying.

Needing him to go, I pleaded, "I am perfectly okay, I promise. You need to go save him. The clock is ticking, and if you don't leave now, you'll lose him for good. I'm sure you don't want to have to live with that."

I purposely played with his conscience, but I hoped it would spur him into action. His eyes squeezed tightly as he reached down for his weapon. Reaching into his pocket, he pulled out a wad of cash and what appeared to be a hotel keycard. "Call a cab and go to the hotel. This is our room card. Address is on the other side. Stay in the suite and lock the door until I get back." Thinking for a second, he added, "Do you have your cell on you?"

"No. It got thrown on the ground in the parking garage below and shattered after Char called, divulging my only means of communication to you guys."

Digging into his other pocket, he pulled out his cell and switched it on. "Here. Take this. I have my military one on me. I'll call you to keep you updated if I can. Call room service and order some food. Take a shower and get cleaned up. We'll get you some clothes when we can."

Reaching into the waistband of his military pants, he pulled out a handgun and pushed it toward me.

"Take this. Shoot first and ask questions later. I mean it, Mac. There may be more enemies approaching or waiting outside."

Glaring at the black metal, knowing it could snuff out a human in the blink of an eye, I hesitated. I'd never used a gun.

"Mac. Look at me."

Rising to meet his concerned eyes, he said, "Life

or death, remember. Leaving you to go to the hotel without me is dishonoring my vow to Dec to keep you safe. I need to know you'll use it if you need to. Time's running out. If I have any chance at all of saving him, I need your promise."

Deciding I was responsible for wasting valuable time, I nodded and grabbed the gun.

While I hated the thought of bailing while he went after Harley, I knew I needed to let him do his job. I'd only slow him down. His kindness spoke volumes about his character.

"Thank you. Truly. For everything." I took the cell in my other hand and pocketed it. He kept his hand on my arm and walked me out of the room, gun trained forward ready to shoot.

***

Back at the hotel after a short cab ride, I locked and dead-bolted the door before hurrying to the bathroom. Placing the gun on the vanity, I almost collapsed with relief, yet fear and worry dug deeper. Outside the warehouse, I'd clung to the walls like a shadow, waiting on someone in hiding to shoot me, but all had remained quiet. Two dead bodies at the back door had failed to push me over the edge. In some ways I'd been relieved. I wanted vengeance on those who had brought this crap into my life.

I desperately needed some hot water to scald away remnants of the animal's dirty hands on me. I'd been violated and abused, and it all began to hit me now. I placed Viper's cell on the vanity next to the gun, which remained ready to shoot. I'd been clutching onto the phone's silence like a lifeline since he'd given it to me, waiting on word that he'd saved Harley, but it remained quiet.

Peeling off my scrubs, I switched the faucets on and climbed into the shower, sinking to the floor under the cathartic spray. Surges of overwhelming sadness barreled through me as the adrenalin subsided and the magnitude of what I'd endured made sense in my head.

Deep heaves shook my chest as the water cascaded over me. I released loud sobs and let myself curl up and sag onto the slowly warming tiles.

The massive beating drum behind my rib cage stole my breath with its intense pounding, the beats jumping every so often from anxiety-fueled palpitations. Visions of evil shone like beacons behind my closed eyelids. Disturbed eyes chock-full of hate as if I'd been the one to kill his brother.

It'd witnessed no empathy or compassion for human life and I wondered how anyone could become so cold and calculated.

Huddling into myself I cried tears of grief and loss. I'd never be the same again. I'd lost a part of myself in the warehouse and perhaps even before that. Who could I trust now?

My close friends and family. Viper, Char, and Harley.

Switching thought patterns, my heart began to bleed for the man who'd put it all on the line for me without so much as a moment's hesitation. And now, his life had been turned over to the asshole who had left a permanent imprint on my psyche.

His torment would be far greater than my own, death being the outcome. I couldn't live with myself if he died. A certain amount of guilt would ride my shoulders for eternity, regardless of whether I had any say in his sacrificial offering.

I don't know how long I lay on the shower floor mulling over everything. The water began to go cold, so I rose like a zombie and dried off, checking the phone again and finding nothing.

Wrapping myself in a hotel robe, I walked out to the bed and crawled on top, still grasping Viper's cell. I stared at it, willing it to ring, my nauseated stomach overturning continuously.

What if he never came home? The moments we'd shared but a flicker in time. Just as I began to dream that maybe I'd found what I'd been looking for all along, it had been snatched away like a terrible tease.

God, I needed him to be all right. He'd been through too much already to have it end this way. His handsome face held firm in my mind's eye as I eventually drifted off.

Chapter Fifteen

Harley

Would I ever see her again? I tried to push images of her distraught face away as footsteps raced up to me from behind. Turning marginally, my hopes of it being the cavalry disappeared when the two men who'd been aiming their weapons at us only a few seconds earlier narrowed the gap. One had his weapon trained on me and the other covered the retreating hallway, walking backward. If I'd been on top of my game I could have taken out the ring-leader before his minions showed up, but I'd been too busy grieving the loss of Mac.

Straightening up, I barely had time to refocus when a blow to the back of the head dropped me to the dusty floor. I never felt the impact because darkness seized me first.

***

Rousing groggily, awareness seeped in. My body

curled awkwardly as if I were inside something. A crate?

Squinting my eyes open, I fought against the surrounding darkness. My head felt like it could explode at any second as agony ripped through my skull. Had I hit my head? A rumble from underneath brought me to life a little quicker. I attempted to sit up, but a metal barrel to my forehead pushed me back down.

"Don't move!" a male voice yelled. My mind had a hard time playing catch up, but instantaneously a barrage of scenes and images flooded my brain, causing me to inhale sharply. Lightheadedness had me loll my head to the side of whatever caged me in. Random events played out in fast motion in no particular order.

Sitting in a classroom with what appeared to be middle-schoolers, passing notes to a boy I recognized as my friend. Danny Burgess. We'd become friends at the beginning of that year and stuck together until high school when he moved away. His red hair and crooked front tooth somehow worked in the overall scheme of his freckled face.

War torn buildings, bombed and crumbling, the smell of gunfire singeing my already sensitive nostrils. Reno, Viper, and my team on alert as we entered a small Afghan village, vacant and beyond repair, searching for survivors on a peace-keeping mission. A young voice, sniveling and pathetic clung to the air as we stepped over the threshold of the remains of a simple slum. Roof blown off and walls crumbling, the meek cry for help took us by surprise. I glanced at Viper and Reno, and they waved their guns to the sound of the child. Rubble and remnants of cheap furniture littered what once would have been a living area. I scanned the space, waiting for another sound.

Sobs mixed with desperation came at me again, and this time, I pinpointed my target. An overturned table in the corner of the room shielded the frightened victim of war. Dragging the wooden structure away, my eyes focused on a small form, huddled and shaking against the wall. I couldn't make out the gender from all the dirt covering the youngster. At a guess I'd say boy, perhaps five or six years old. Abandoned and left to die. My steely heart wasn't immune to the ravages and tragedies of war, especially when children were involved. They didn't ask to be born. They didn't ask to have such adversity thrust upon them. And this youngster who'd be mentally scarred forever, with no shoes and matted dirty hair, scared beyond belief, made me take pause. Sorrow filled me. The child should be attending school, laughing with friends, instead of cowering in the remnants of his bombed house, alone and worrying we'd come to finish him off. His small head turned, his eyes round with dread. I held up my hand and dropped my weapon, crouching to put myself on a more even keel.

Flattening himself further against the wall in the hopes it would swallow him up, guilt and disgust riddled me. Both converged together in a powerful slap to my ego. In a moment of clarity, I became ashamed of the human race. We were doing this to *ourselves because of greed, race, religion, and money. How had everything become so screwed up?*

Another flash. Jumbled images twisted and turned. Faces and places. My mother and father. My dad before he died. His funeral. My childhood dog, Zep, short for Zeppelin, grinning as we ran through the park on a Sunday morning just around the corner from home. Smells bombarded me. A summer shower of rain settling into a garden filled with roses caught me as we tore past Mrs. Shepherd's dated Victorian. Mom's blueberry pancakes seeping into the yard through the open window as I kicked off my sneakers near the porch. Her perfume grabbing me and holding as I charged at her for a hug, with Zep riding my tails.

With the mental movie came an overwhelming influx of emotions. An onslaught almost too much to contend with. I retched weakly, my stomach deciding it couldn't handle the excess acid formed by the return of my memory in one fell swoop.

A few loud pops outside failed to drag me out of my speeding movie, which entrenched me within its confines. My overloaded senses were dragged from past to present and back again, never lingering long.

The fire in my skull raged, pain shooting from the top of my scalp to the top of my spine. Something told me my sudden memory recall had been brought about by blunt force trauma.

The contents of my stomach rose, and as I heaved again, I brought everything up in the small space I occupied. More vertigo seized me, taking me once again into the nothing.

***

This time when I came to, my body wasn't folded in on itself. My legs and arms rested comfortably on a soft surface.

Voices cut into the quiet.

"He's coming around."

"He took quite a blow to the head. You think he'll be okay?"

"I hope so. I'm just happy he's alive. You saved him."

"Told you I would."

Whispered words followed by, "Thank you."

I know that voice. Her voice. Please don't be a dream! Am I dead this time? Don't tease me. Make it real. Make her real.

Opening my eyes, her puffy, bruised face came into view, bringing a snarl from my throat at the recollection of what had gone down. I moved to sit up, but fell back down as dizziness slapped me, hard. More fragments of my subconscious filtered through, and then like a roaring train with no brakes, I hurtled into my own head with its infinite flashes. Bits and pieces of the jigsaw puzzle thrown in a pile for me to sort out. A soft hand came to my arm in comfort but I shucked it away, overcome by my brain's overload. A collection of events from birth to present vying for space, some horrific, some amazing. With each unlocked piece of my past came the emotions that sat with the occasion. Fear. Love. Wonder. Hatred. Self-loathing. Worry. Joy. All of it together but unsorted, filling the void at an alarming rate.

"Fuck!" I roared, gripping my scalp. I just wanted it to stop. Make it stop!

"Harley?" her soft voice rose in concern, but I couldn't shake my waking nightmare. I couldn't quite grasp onto the comfort it always brought me. I floundered, drowning.

I'd killed people. Seen things. Horrific things. Bodies mutilated. Heads blown off. Friends dead in my arms. Reno...God. Reno! Guilt pulled me under.

A shadow loomed. The enemy. I lashed out, flailing my fists, not concerned about the wounded cry or the semi-focused image of my beautiful nurse. I howled in pain. Not physical, but mental. Scars cut so deep, stitched back together haphazardly.

"Dec, man! Stop! You hurt Mac. Calm down!" Large hands pushed my shoulders down into the mattress.

I shook my head, my body already trembling. Tears fell down my face as I squeezed my eyes tightly, attempting to purge the horror of who I was and what I'd done. What I'd seen.

"Dec. You're safe. It's okay. Open your eyes." Viper. My wingman. My battle buddy. The only one who knew the torment, beneath. He'd lived it too. Right by my side.

"Shhh. Come on, dude. Don't do this. Come back." His dusty voice begged with a level of authority that made me blink several times and focus. It took a moment as I swiped at the tears.

My vision showed not a warzone but a room. I saw the concern in his green eyes as I let him settle

131

me. "You okay? Shit." Letting me go, he backed off, allowing my sight to move across the room. My eyes pinned Mac, standing on the other side of my bed, holding her arm. Fuck! Had I done that? I didn't mean to. I'd never hurt her intentionally. And yet, she stood frightened, half the woman she had been when I'd first met her. God, her marred face. The wounds raw and blatant. I did that. I caused all of it. A beautiful, tragic mess. Not directly, but indirectly, and that had proved just as bad. I'd never get over hurting her and she'd never begin to understand why. No one could possibly understand my grief. Her fear made me feel pathetic and weak. She may not admit it but right now, but she was scared of me. And so she should be. I wasn't who she'd created. Harley. The guy deserving of such a woman. The guy I'd wanted to be for her. The guy I could no longer be.

The strong, independent woman who had promised to stick by me until my memories returned now cowered like a mouse. Afraid. Of. Me.

Her wide eyes held mine with pity and fright. She made no move to come closer. The room began to swallow me up with her reaction. I fought to remain focused on her as my brain caught and held more memories. Memories of the person I'd always been but had lost. And the person I had become under Mac's care dangled in limbo, neither here nor there. I didn't know what to do with him. He was me, yet he wasn't. He was what she wanted and needed. Dec would hurt her. The damaged soldier. I couldn't wake up each day seeing the same hesitation in her eyes. Wondering if each day would bring another meltdown.

I knew what I needed to do. To save her I needed to hurt her. She had no business being caught up in my mess. I would fail her. Not physically, but emotionally. Now that I knew everything, my nightmare had only just begun. I needed help. I had to let her go and fix myself.

Saving her life had been just the beginning. Now I needed to save her soul.

Masking my emotions, I gripped the sheet and ground out, "Leave. Now. I don't need you here."

Nothing could be further from the truth, but if she stayed, she'd witness someone I didn't want her to see. The real me. A soldier with a fucked up brain caused by war.

Her blue eyes appeared horrified at my command. She looked at Viper for support but he remained silent, eyes slightly squinting as if he were trying to read my change of heart.

"I mean it. You need to leave." My voice held the authority I now remembered as being a commanding officer's.

I needed to punch something. To release the valve that had my head constricted so tightly. I could barely breathe without screaming.

Her weak voice asked, "Where will I go?"

Drinking in more of the bedroom I lay in, I realized it belonged to the hotel we had rented. She couldn't very well go home because we weren't in Ann Arbor.

"Just go out in the living area," I barked.

Viper moved to go too, but I lurched forward, gripping his wrist as he pulled away. "You. Stay."

I didn't wait to see Mac disappear. I felt detached. Wrong. My vision blurred. A flash of the small boy huddling in the Afghani town plagued me along with one of our crew being shot through the head in an attack from militant rebels. Any peaceful memories of family and friends took a backseat. Violence and carnage shot to the fore. Bloodshed. Death.

"Make it stop!" Squeezing my eyes tightly, I pounded on my temple with my fist, needing something to numb me.

"Dec. What's happening?"

"Brain overload. All the images from our tours. I can't shake them. All of them." I could only hear Viper's voice come closer with my eyes closed.

"I'm calling 000."

I didn't damn well care. I just needed a clear head.

I vaguely heard him make the call.

"They're on their way."

Nodding and dragging in deep breaths, I attempted to fight the deluge. "Mac. Make sure she's okay."

He perched on the edge of the bed as I opened my eyes. "What was that about before? She's gone through hell and you virtually yelled at her to get the fuck out." He spoke genuinely. I knew he liked Mac. He could tell she made me happy. Normally. When I knew nothing about my past. When I wasn't Declan Harding.

Hissing out a breath between my teeth, I propped myself up on the pillow, not knowing how to explain, but figuring if anyone would understand, it would be Viper. Staring at him, trying to remain present, feeling the sheets underneath me and letting the smells of the room keep me grounded, I hoped I could help him see.

"Harley's the guy she met. He's the one she knows. In light of what I know now and what I've been through, I don't know if I can be him anymore. My head is a mess. I feel like I'm going crazy. I want to physically tear someone apart from the infinite rage coursing through me. Jesus, Viper. How did you do it? Get through it all, I mean."

He'd been there with me. Seen the same things. Probably had the same shit going over and over in his head. And yet, he seemed so put together. Thinking back through the muck sinking my mind, I searched for memories of my friend having a meltdown at any stage but he answered the question for me.

"It wasn't easy. Cost me my girl. The one I had asked to marry me."

Gripping the blanket covering me and squeezing it as more images tried to steal me back, I jiggled my legs and slowed my breathing.

Ahh, yeah. The house he'd brought as a family home. The memory peeked through. Cindy.

"She left because of your drinking and anger."

Folding his arms across his chest, clearly uncomfortable, he grunted. "I had it all. Career. Home. Woman I loved. Then it all went to hell after the second tour. I totally lost my shit."

He had. I'd nearly lost him as a friend because of it. He'd derailed, drowning himself in bottles of Jack Daniels. The only thing that had pulled him back from the edge had been medication and counseling.

"The thing with you is, you've got everything flooding your brain all at once. I had the shit happen over time. You're trying to process it all now. It sucks for you. You need something to help with that. I'm telling you, the meds they put me on are what helped me get up each morning."

Feeling another wave of daytime drama appearing in my mind, I hung my head, attempting to push it back. There were no triggers. It just happened rapidly. Randomly.

A knock sounded on the door before it opened and two medics appeared, Mac in the background looking flustered and stressed. My heart called out to her but I didn't need to be dealing with more emotional stuff right now. I couldn't think past my own anxiety. She'd understand. I didn't want to lose her, but the vermin in my psyche twisted and twirled like sharp claws. The suddenly new version of myself felt detached from her as if Harley had all been a dream.

Chapter Sixteen

Mac

Harley had woken from his head trauma with his full memory. How did I react to that? He wasn't the make-believe Harley any more. Harley had been nothing more than a pretend version of Declan. A temporary persona. Watching him process his memories, mainly bad, had cut me to the bone. I wanted to help but clearly he didn't need it. He chose the friend who'd seen him through thick and thin. And why should it be any other way? I'd only known him for such a short time. He didn't owe me a thing. And I shouldn't hope for anything more.

Already in too deep, if he asked me to walk away and never see him again, it would gut me. Just going into another room and leaving him vulnerable had been hard enough. Or had his order a double meaning? Perhaps he had meant for me to leave and never come back. His voice had sounded so final. I'd been there for him right up until a few moments ago and the idea of not being wanted anymore had my stress level at an unhealthy high. Harley had the ability to break me.

Maybe he needed time to pull himself together. To let his past settle into some sort of order. He must be going through hell, and it was selfish of me to be considering my own feelings.

I'd seen PTSD patients at the hospital. They carried a heavy burden. Sometimes too much to handle. We always referred them to a clinical psychologist. Fingers crossed Harley would be given the same option. *Harley*. It now sounded foreign. Harley had never existed. He'd always been Declan. A person I'd never known. A life I'd never been a part of. Suddenly I felt like an outsider. Is that how he saw me now?

I'd let the paramedics in and they loaded him onto the gurney, injecting a liquid into his arm that seemed to sedate him somewhat. His eyes glassed over and his lids struggled to remain open. His bleary eyes found mine as they wheeled him past.

He mumbled something but I only caught, "Mac."

I wanted to go with him. One of the medics stopped when he saw me.

"Are you okay, Ma'am? Do you need medical treatment also?"

Viper hadn't taken me to the hospital in light of him needing to rescue Harley. I'd almost forgotten about my face. They must wonder what I'd been involved in.

"No. I'm fine. I got into a fight but, ah…it's been handled. Thank you."

He stared at me for a few long seconds before

nodding and taking Harley out. Walking to Viper, I asked, "Can I go too? I need to be with him even if he doesn't want me there."

He didn't hesitate. "Of course. I'll bring you back with me later."

Grateful to have him here, I stepped closer and hugged him, needing the contact after Harley's attempt at pushing me away.

His arms didn't immediately embrace me, but after a beat or two they came around my waist in a firm squeeze.

"He'll come around," he muttered softly.

I could only hope.

***

For some reason being in a hospital this time unnerved me. Funny, considering I spent most of my time in one. It differed, being a hopeful and concerned friend, waiting in an overcrowded room, unable to hurry the process or see what went on behind the closed door facing us.

"You want a coffee?" Viper asked.

"Please," I replied, grateful for his thoughtfulness. Watching him walk away, I felt helpless.

I hadn't seen Harley since he'd been wheeled out of the hotel room. Viper and I traveled behind the ambulance up until a point, where we'd veered off to do a detour, but then had to gain access like regular civilians to the ER waiting room. I couldn't stop thinking of the way he'd forced me from the hotel bedroom. His heated stare. Angry. Did he really feel animosity toward me or was it more a case of him protecting me by pushing me away? Either way, it hurt. I'd been through my own trauma, and having him throw me out like garbage added insult to injury. What an absolutely crappy twenty-four hours.

On the way we'd done a quick stop at a clothing store to pick me up some clothes. My scrubs I'd been abducted in were a mess, and we figured we had half an hour up our sleeve at least until paperwork for Harley had been filled out.

Viper soon returned with my coffee. We sat in silence for a bit, so I decided to help pass the time and get my mind off Harley by finding out more about him. I really didn't know a lot. Harley hadn't divulged much, and with everything going on, I hadn't thought to ask.

Not knowing how much of his personal life he wanted to share, I started with, "So. How come you haven't got the ladies chasing you?" It seemed a fair question. I hadn't heard any mention of a girlfriend and he lived alone.

Turning to slant me a quick glance, he spun back to his coffee. He didn't respond right away and used the military excuse. "Don't really have time for one. I'm away a lot."

It felt like a cop out. There were plenty of military wives out there who made it work. Perhaps he'd had a bad relationship or two and preferred being single.

"So you've never had a long relationship?" Curiosity made me push a little.

Swigging his coffee, he shrugged his shoulders

and gave me another brief look. "You're a nosy little thing, aren't you?"

"Just curious."

Sighing, he tightened his grip on his cup. "I had someone special a while back. We were engaged to be married. I bought her a house." Clearing his throat, he hung his head, pausing. Suddenly I felt bad for prying.

"I'm sorry. You don't have to talk about it." I gave him an out.

"Let's just say I thought she was the one. It damn near killed me when she left."

Downing the rest of his coffee, he rose to toss the cup in the trash nearby. When he circled back and walked to his seat, lines etched his brow and his lips had compressed.

Nothing more was spoken.

When it felt like we'd been sitting there for hours, Viper went to the triage nurse and asked about Harley. After a few minutes we were told we could go see him. As much as he probably didn't want to see me, I needed him to know I couldn't be pushed away so easily.

Upon entering the ER, we were led past a nurses' station and around the corner to a curtained room, lined up against others. A child cried and a loud groan echoed through the other hospital noise. I knew the sounds well.

Pushing open the curtain to reveal Harley, the nurse shut it again to give us some privacy. Harley's eyes opened when we moved to his bedside.

Pain bled from his eyes. His vulnerable state allowed me to see through the tough exterior and into the real man. My heart stuttered. What went through his head? If I didn't know better, I'd think his emotions were aimed at me. Perhaps they were. Perhaps he'd decided with me in the picture, he'd always feel the need to put his own life on the line.

Maybe he didn't want that anymore.

His anger toward me earlier still hurt. I shouldn't take it personally with my knowledge on PTSD, but how could I not? He'd told me to leave. He didn't want me near him. But his focus on me now told a different story. He appeared confused and remorseful.

I stopped and let Viper move forward, remaining in the background to keep my distance.

Chapter Seventeen

Harley

When Mac appeared through the hospital curtain drawn around my bed, it took me by surprise. Especially after the way I'd barked at her to leave the hotel room. I expected her to run and never look back, but here she stood. Still gorgeous even with a swollen, bruised face. Her eyes still held a wariness toward me I'd put there earlier. Part of me hated myself for hurting her, and the other part knew it needed to happen to keep her safe. From myself. The pure white hot rage that still rocketed through me, held firm. She couldn't be around me. I'd break her even more than she was after the attack. I knew Viper flanked her, but I didn't acknowledge him. I pierced her with a look I hoped let her know I hadn't changed my mind. God. In all honesty, I wanted to pull her to me and never let go, but until I got my emotions under control I couldn't risk hurting her again. She probably had bruises on her arm from my episode at the hotel when I lashed out.

It gutted me to see the fear in her eyes. She held back, almost afraid to come closer. So when I opened my mouth, the words that came out killed me.

"What are you doing here? I told you to leave," I bit out, shame filling me.

I swear I thought I heard her heart crack some more and I had to look away. I found Viper's angry stare on me. He looked like he wanted to knock some sense into me.

"She came to see how you were doing because she cares, but I can see you're still being an asshole."

No one spoke to me like that and got away with it except Viper. He could be fierce when needed and could hold his own both in a physical and verbal fight. He only ever had my best interests at heart, so I respected him madly. Still, he needed to be put in his place too.

"I made it perfectly clear what I wanted earlier and nothing has changed."

Turning to her, I choked on my words. "Go. Wait outside."

Her glassy eyes kicked me in the stomach and I hated myself even more in that moment. One day hopefully she'd understand that I'd only done it to protect her.

Her lip trembled as she whispered, "I just wanted to make sure you were okay."

She held my gaze for a moment and then turned to Viper. "I'll wait near the nurses' station."

Giving her a smile, he offered, "I won't be long."

She probably hated me now. And so she should.

I was a dick.

When we were alone, I knew my friend would lay into me.

"Jesus! Can you stop pushing her away? She truly cares, man, and if you're not careful, you'll lose her. Personally, I think she's the best thing to ever happen to you, but for some strange reason you've changed your tune."

He reached over and pulled a metal chair from the corner and sat next to my bed. His face looked drawn. He'd suffered by having my back too and I could see the worry in his eyes.

"I don't want to hurt her."

"You're hurting her more by being an ass." He crossed one leg over the thigh of the other and glared at me.

I hated his scrutiny. He knew me better than anyone and could probably read into my bullshit and why I pushed Mac away.

Scratching his head, he added, "Look. I get that you feel overwhelmed with the influx of memories. Especially the ones of war. I still have nightmares. It's not easy by any means, but I think Mac will cope just fine. She's a nurse, for God's sake. She's dealt with screwed up people. She knows what to do."

My eyebrows lifted at his praise of the woman I had fallen for. It warmed me that he cared so much. With Trudy, he had never taken to her. He'd stumbled through his role of best man at my wedding to appease me. We'd argued in the past about his dislike for her, but in the end his distaste had been close to the mark when she'd screwed

Reno.

"What?" he asked.

"You like her."

"Hell yeah. She's a great girl and I think you owe her the chance to prove to you she can handle your shit."

Rubbing my face, I took a deep breath and let it out slowly. "Looking at her face all banged up sends me into a rage. I just want to dismember that fucker. Even though he did that to her physically, I'm responsible."

"You didn't ask for any of it either. So stop beating yourself up and let her help."

Unable to cope with the conversation, I steered it in a different direction. Remembering Viper hadn't filled me in on the outcome of our mission to save Mac, I asked him, "What happened after I was taken and knocked out?"

Viper grinned almost manically. "I took him and his two goons out."

Relief filled me. The immediate threat had gone. I wondered if they had any other members of their group to take over their task of hunting me down and killing me. Giving him a brief nod, I needed any information on why our soldiers hadn't backed us up after the code had been sent.

"You probably haven't had time to look into why our team failed to act?"

"I'll get onto it soon. I've been taking care of your girl."

"Thank you. I mean it. I'm glad she has you."

"I've got your back. Always. Just so glad to have you here." He paused briefly to change topics.

"Sooo…how's the head?"

"Not feeling so overwhelmed by thoughts after the jab the medic gave me, but I feel so damn angry and I can't get past it."

"It's the PTSD. You'll calm down once you've been taking meds for a bit. Trust me. It gets better." Even as he said it, I could see he didn't believe his own words. Still, I had enough to deal with.

I huffed. "I need to get out of here and get back to my apartment. Think you can organize it?"

"On one condition."

Here we go. "What's that?"

"You stop being a dick and talk to Mac. At least tell her why you're pushing her away. You owe her that."

Feeling like a jerk. I nodded. "Send her in."

Viper left and my nerves shot into the red zone. I'd explain myself. It didn't mean I could put her in a position of getting hurt by one of my nightmares or outbursts again. She needed to know I couldn't pursue anything with her until I sorted my crap out. If she chose to wait for the undisclosed amount of time, it would be up to her. I wasn't expecting her to though.

Waiting wasn't something I liked to do. She took forever to push the door open. Seeing her wary, beaten face didn't help my cause.

Watching her quietly pad to the bed and sit down in the chair Viper had pulled over, I knew I needed to apologize. At the very least, she needed to know I still carried a morsel of decency. She needed to know I still cared. I owed her so much damn respect it tore me in two.

"Mac." God. Those eyes. They killed me. Every. Damn. Time.

"I heard Viper talking to the nurse. They're organizing your release."

That voice. The one that had dragged me from the nothingness of my coma. The one that had screamed and pleaded with me not to hand myself over to terrorists to save her. Jesus. My heart was in turmoil over this woman and the choices I needed to make. "That's great. I need to get home."

Seeing her shoulders still tense, I sighed and attempted to explain. "I…uh…I'm sorry about earlier. I'm not pushing you away to be a dick— even though that's what I ended up coming across as." Gaging her stock expression, I continued, "Look. My feelings for you haven't changed. I just think we should throw some distance between us until I get my head back in the game. What happened in the hotel room…me hitting you…I can't ever do that again. I don't want to hurt you."

I didn't know what else to say or how to say it.

Her features softened somewhat at my attempt to justify my actions.

"I don't need protecting. Not from you. I know you'd never intentionally hurt me. I understand what you're going through. It's going to take time. And medication. You need to take the meds the nurse will give you to take home. It'll help with the anger. I also think you need to go talk to someone. I can arrange it through University Hospital. I'm here to help, Harley. Please don't push me away." Reaching across, she placed her hand over mine.

Harley. That name again. The one she chose for

me. A man who had taken on the moniker under false pretenses. During my amnesia I'd basked in the name because she'd given it to me. I never wanted to be Declan. But the fact was, now that I felt every morsel of emotion, good and bad, and had emerged from my cocoon, I couldn't help but be him. Unable to correct her, I bit my tongue for now.

My skin sizzled at her touch. A deep longing drew forth along with the dread that I'd be unable to stop myself from hurting her. I didn't pull away though. I let the feel of her skin soothe my insecurities.

Staring at her, I wondered if she had the strength to help me fight my battles. Her job would always come first. The hours she worked were long and tiresome. I couldn't always guarantee that I'd be what she needed.

"Mac. I want to give you the world. I want to be the man you've never had but have always wanted. It's just…" How did I get through to her? I didn't know what the hell went through my head.

She widened her eyes expectantly.

"I don't think I'm enough at the moment."

That didn't even come out right. Christ. Pulling my hand out from hers, I turned and faced the window.

"You can tell yourself that and you can even tell me that, but I don't believe you. How about you let me be the judge of that?"

Her words sounded hard. They caught my attention enough to turn back around and face her. I had to admit…the woman had guts. I'd always known she had immense strength. That's one of the things I loved about her. Loved? The epiphany slammed into me. Hard. I actually think I loved her. Enough so, that I needed to make sure I lived up to her expectations. I had to set her free to become the man she deserved. It didn't matter that she felt I was that man now. I knew I wasn't.

"I appreciate you and everything you've done for me. I wouldn't have made it if not for your kindness. Taking me into your home. Feeding and clothing me. Risking your life for me. Don't you see? It's all been you. You've done everything for me. All I've done for you is bring danger to your door. Literally."

"It's okay…"

Cutting her off, I continued. "Let me finish. I stand by my decision to get my shit in order. You need to get on with things and forget about me for a while. I need time to process everything."

Hurt drew her brows together, but she didn't argue any further. She simply nodded, mouth tight. Resigned to the fact.

We didn't have any time for more discussion because Viper appeared through the door with a doctor in tow.

He handed me a script. "You need to keep taking these meds. They'll help with the overwhelming sensation you're experiencing and also the flashes. You'll be on them for a while, so make sure you don't skip any days."

Taking it from him, I nodded.

"You can leave anytime you're ready. You appear to have stabilized. We injected you with something to help for the next few hours, but it's important you begin the tablets I just gave you when you get home."

"Thank you," I offered, waiting on him to leave before rising off the bed.

I wobbled a little, but Viper moved in quickly to steady me.

"You okay?" he asked.

"Yeah. All good. I just want to get out of here. Do you think we can head back to Ann Arbor soon?"

"We can go pick up our stuff and drive home if that's what you want. You can crash at my place for a few days if you need to until your meds kick in."

I wasn't sure I wanted to be around anyone, but then again, being alone in my apartment mightn't be the best either. If I needed an outlet to vent, at least Viper could handle me. Unlike Mac. Speaking of which, I knew she waited outside. We'd be traveling back home together. It would be more than awkward. Had I made the right decision in letting her go for now?

What if she found someone else? The idea killed me. Would she wait?

Everything was so screwed up.

Chapter Eighteen

Mac

We'd arrived back home an hour ago. Viper dropped me off before he and Harley left. Not before they'd double-checked my apartment and made sure I would be okay. After everything we'd been through they were simply being thorough. I actually liked it. I knew Viper at least cared. He acted all tough on the outside, but deep down he had a big heart to those he cared about. He'd do anything for Harley, and for that I would always be grateful.

The ride home had been tense. Few spoken words and lots of grunts and sighs. I'd dozed for a short while, overcome by the weight of my ordeal.

It felt great being back in my apartment, although Harley's absence left a gaping hole.

When I'd walked into the bedroom, Nick's things had all been removed. He'd obviously returned and taken his clothing and personal items. All the furniture remained. Part of me felt saddened at his departure, knowing how it had ended, but the other part sagged with relief. I no longer had to worry about whether he'd be coming home from work at some ungodly hour or if he would even eat with me. Still, a part of my life had ended and I didn't take it lightly.

Because I had no cell, I gave the boys my home number so I could be contacted. I'd need to replace it later in the day. Viper had also promised to return my car from the hospital parking lot where it had been sitting since my abduction. I hoped it hadn't been stolen or scratched in any way. My baby.

Now that Harley wasn't responsible for my safety any longer, I didn't need to move out. I could stay in the apartment as long as I wanted. Looking for somewhere else to live didn't carry the same enthusiasm it had before. Everything I owned was here.

I called the hospital and they agreed to give me a week off. Turning up looking like a victim of domestic violence would not be taken well by my patients. Grateful for the time to rest, I sent Char an email from my computer to give her an update before running a tub of steaming water and sinking into it.

With nothing to do but think, my mind began a loop of images. The manic face, grinning at me and dirty fingers groping in places they shouldn't. A gun trained at my back and head, the cold metal branding me with the threat of death.

Up until now, it had all seemed like a horrible nightmare. With suffocating silence, the reality of it came tumbling down. I almost died. Harley had almost died. I'd been kidnapped from a busy hospital from under the noses of my colleagues. I'd been a part of some terrorist's revenge plot.

Foreign emotions surfaced, rapidly threatening to drown me in the shallow bath water. The past twenty-four hours could never be undone. The images would haunt me forever. My hands shook as I gripped my head and sobbed hard. My chest weighed two tons, my heart even more.

The idea of being a hair's breadth away from death strangled me. The final morsel of strength left me on a rushed wail, my limbs wilting in defeat. My face smarted with the battle my body waged. My eye was all but closed, and felt ten times puffier than it probably was.

The bathroom carried my heaving voice around its four walls, bouncing it back to me like a boomerang. Alone. I felt so alone. I just needed to be held and soothed and told everything would be all right. To let go and have someone else be my strength for a change. I'd held it together pretty well in the dusty warehouse, but now I crumbled into tiny pieces.

My own harsh sobs rang in my ears. The hot water failed to warm me as I shuddered. I felt so damn miserable, locked in a battle with my brain and my emotions.

The solitude amplified everything. Bringing my knees up to my chest, I wrapped my arms around them, resting my forehead on top.

This happened to others. Not me. Not safe, reliable Mac. Somebody who was always there for others but never truly there for herself. My brain switched gears over and over, playing out what had happened and what could have happened. Every scent. Every sound. Every click of a gun and clack of a boot on floorboards. How could people turn so evil? I'd stared Satan directly in the face and been revolted by his manic enjoyment over my torment.

Gagging, I laid my head on the back of the tub, attempting to refrain from vomiting. I breathed. In. Out. In. Out. Until the acid lowered back into my stomach from my throat. My chest ached from crying so much, but I couldn't move. The cooling water held me captive, only mildly comforting. The small bathroom space offered a refuge as if the four walls might keep me safe.

Not sure how long I stayed like that, purging my soul. I startled when someone pounded on the bathroom door. What the hell? How did someone get in my house? I'd locked the front door. Hadn't I?

"Mac. It's me. Are you all right? Answer me, damn it!" A rich, thunderous voice.

Harley? What was he doing here? Viper had agreed to return my car. I couldn't let him see me like this. A mess. He'd already taken responsibility for putting me in harm's way. To know I'd succumbed to its clutches would push him further away.

Hearing the fear in his voice, I called out. "Yes. I'm okay. How did you get in?"

"When you didn't answer the front door, I got worried. I picked the lock."

Of course he did. "Give me a moment. I'll be out in a minute."

He sounded worried. Did that mean he still cared? He'd told me as much but I just didn't know anymore.

Hearing him trudge down the hallway, I stood and let the water out of the tub, reaching for a towel and drying off.

Attempting to pull myself together, I checked the mirror to find a monster looking back. The bruising had well and truly begun to set in and puffiness mixed with bloodshot eyes had transformed me into something from *The Walking Dead*. My shoulders drooped, wondering if that's the real reason Harley had pushed me away. He couldn't stand to look at me. In a way, that was true because it did remind him of his part in everything. I didn't blame him though. How could I? Neither of us knew just what he'd been involved with and how it would come back to bite him.

Taking a few deep breaths, not wanting to reveal my meltdown, I stepped out into the hallway, expecting him to be tucked away in the living room out of sight, waiting for me. With my head to the ground, I walked into his solid body, crashing my head against his chest. He barely moved as his arms came up to steady me.

"Shit!" I let loose. "You scared me!"

"Easy, angel."

Viper appeared in the hallway. "Everything okay?"

Glancing from Harley back to Viper, I replied, "Yes. I'm fine. I was soaking in the tub. That's why I didn't hear you knocking."

Viper looked appeased but Harley was far from

it. He stared at me. Unforgiving. Gripping my jaw on either side, he forced my head up. "What's wrong? You've been crying."

I wanted to reply with, "What do you care?" but I held my tongue, fearful that I might start weeping again. My tears had barely dried. My dry throat hurt, causing me to swallow consecutively.

He leaned down slightly at eye level, his scent wafting over me. I needed his arms around me in comfort but I daren't ask. Not when he'd so boldly told me how he felt.

All I could manage was, "What are you doing here, Harley?"

"We brought your car back. Viper needed me to drive yours. It's parked in the driveway."

"Thank you." It came out dry and husky from my meltdown.

For a moment he looked confused with what he should do next, but after a deep breath he enfolded me within the safety of his oversized arms.

I couldn't help it. I cried some more, unable to stop. I'd never wept so much, and after sobbing for ages in the tub, it surprised me I still had anything left in reserve.

For whatever reason he let his guard down and held me, it didn't matter. I took the moment for what it was, needing the comfort it brought. His solid frame acted as a barrier of protection, his generous arms, the locks to ensure my safety. I relished in the feel they brought, not caring if they were temporary.

"Shhh. It's okay. You're safe now."

He knew. He damn well knew. I didn't need to

say a word. His lips rested on the side of my face as his tone soothed me, the whispered words vibrating against my skin.

"I can't stop crying."

"You've been through quite an ordeal. I'm not surprised. Just let it all out." Calm Harley had returned. For how long, I didn't know, but I held on, needing the support. His arms remained solid and safe, and I didn't want to leave their confines. Ever. But after a moment, I could feel him tense up again as he took a step back.

"You need anything?"

As if flicking a switch, he returned to indifferent mode. Frustrated, knowing he thought he was doing it to protect me from himself, I shuffled away toward the kitchen.

He didn't follow immediately, but then after a beat or two I heard his boots heavy on the floor. When I reached the kitchen, I met Viper just stepping out. "Coffee? Tea? Scotch?" he asked with a slight smirk.

Coughing out a laugh, I shook my head. "No. Thank you. I'm good now."

He shot a heated look to Harley. "One of us is staying here tonight. You gonna volunteer?"

Butting in, I cried out, "No! It's okay. I had a meltdown, that's all. I'm fine now, really."

He shook his head. "Not happening, darlin'."

I swung to Harley to see what his answer would be. He stood rigid, arms tight into his body.

"Fine," he ground out, not looking at me.

"That's settled then. I'm heading home. I'll call around tomorrow to pick up douche over there."

Glancing at his watch, he added, "You still got that cell I gave you, Dec?" He jerked his head in the direction of his friend, who gave a curt nod. With that he walked to me, gave me a brief hug, and whispered, "Call me if he gets too much." Then he left, leaving me perplexed with his organization of everything. Why had he volunteered Harley to watch over me when he needed as much if not more monitoring? Ugh. My brain couldn't analyze another damn thing.

When the door shut he said, "You should go rest. Catch up on some sleep."

I didn't want to rest. As exhausted as I felt, I knew sleep wouldn't come easily.

"No. I'm going to try and eat something. I haven't had anything for what feels like days." The idea of food had my stomach lurch, but I needed sustenance of some kind to give me some energy.

"Go in the living room. I'll get you something," he barked as if I were one of his soldiers.

Surprised he offered when, judging by the look of him he could drop at any moment, I simply stood and left the kitchen, a numbness blanketing me.

I listened as cupboards opened and shut, cutlery clanged, and water ran. He knew his way around my kitchen and had proven to me he was quite capable. Easing back into the chair, I let him fuss. He'd been put on the spot by his friend and now had to stay here under duress. I needed to give him credit for keeping himself in check to babysit me.

Striding out and placing a plate with a veggie sandwich down, he rubbed the top of his head and looked at the ground as if he didn't know what to do next.

"Thank you. You can sit, you know. I won't bite."

Opting for the chair beside the sofa, he kept his distance, maybe not trusting himself. The air was thick with unsaid things. I'd never been uncomfortable around him before and I didn't like it now.

Grabbing the remote, I flicked the television on to make some noise. Switching channels, I settled on a cooking show and we both sat quietly, me not really watching it. Harley seemed to stare through it.

When I felt myself nodding off a while later, I rose, hating how much silence had passed between us. Harley looked to me with bleary eyes as if he fought sleep himself. I wanted nothing more than to reach out to him. Why could we not comfort each other? We were each fighting our own demons. It would be better to fight them together.

As tired as I was, my sleep would be fraught with the threat of nightmares. Not wanting to be on my own, I said, "I'm going to lie down. I don't think I want to be alone. Please? Stay in my room. At least if I know you're there it might prevent another meltdown."

Closing his eyes briefly and breathing heavily out his nose, he opened them while scrubbing a hand over his face. He appeared torn. "I shouldn't."

"It doesn't have to mean anything. I just want company."

"I thought you said you were fine." He took a step toward me, eyes narrowing.

"I am…I mean…I probably would be…but…" Quite honestly, I knew I was far from fine. What a pair we were. It seemed we both suffered from PTSD.

In a split second he stood, had me by the wrist and dragged me down the hallway to the bedroom. Throwing the door open and kicking it shut with his foot, he drew the curtains and walked to the bed, pulling the covers down.

He began taking his clothes off.

"What are you doing?" I asked, panicked.

"Getting ready for bed."

"In the nude?"

Throwing his jeans, boots, and shirt on the chair in the corner, he hinted at a smile. The first one I'd seen in a while. "I normally sleep in boxers. You okay with that?"

Nodding, words failed me as I took in his fine form. I couldn't help but ogle. Even relaxed, his muscles bulged. Blinking a couple of times, I fought off my stupor as he climbed into bed. I walked to the closet and changed into a tank and long pajama bottoms before switching the light off and lying down on the very edge of the bed on my side, keeping plenty of distance between us. I felt the heat rolling off him and his manly smell, which I inhaled softly so he couldn't hear me. With my eyes open, I lay still listening to him breathing beside me, knowing full well that I'd still be in the same position when naptime ended.

Chapter Nineteen

Harley

Sinking to the ground as gracefully as possible, considering we were all loaded up with armory and weapons, we disengaged our chutes and assembled together. Ammunition hung like expensive, cumbersome jewelry around our necks. We needed to carry it the four miles to reach our destination.

Our peace-keeping mission not only entailed rescuing the innocent, it also involved hostile means of eliminating the enemy.

We had the element of surprise at 3 a.m., shrouded in darkness, our heat-seeking goggles our guides.

We'd aborted radio contact with our base upon touching down in the desert, knowing our intent.

As the commanding officer of the mission, my team trusted me implicitly to give them direction. Some of the men had served on other tours, some not. Either way, they all had my back and I had, theirs. We were a solid unit.

Viper signaled to me that there were no immediate threats and we could proceed. He was always my eyes and ears and had the uncanny ability to hear and see things I couldn't. He'd saved my ass many times with his sharp instincts. I owed him everything.

The trek through the unforgiving terrain of Afghanistan proved difficult in the cloak of night. We moved quietly and cautiously, the dusty wasteland coating our nostrils with minute particles of its landscape. A souvenir sometimes even a long, hot shower failed to eradicate.

Nothing stirred. No sign of life, and why should there be in the middle of Goddam nowhere? I couldn't afford the luxury of thinking about home. My wife and life, separate from my job. I needed my head present and focused no matter how hard switching off could be.

We trudged for another hour, stopping only once to rehydrate. Nearing a rocky outcrop, I knew we were close. Over the other side sat a small village overrun by savage militants we needed to weed out.

Regrouping, we took pause before rounding the bend. My pack of five soldiers, through our coded sign language, would fan out into formation so we could approach the small establishment from all angles.

I waited while they moved away from me, leaving me somewhat vulnerable, but knowing we were ghosts in the night and virtually undetectable.

A hot breeze swept across the barren expanse as I took my first step forward, ready to shoot anyone who tried to attack.

Standing behind a boulder, I moved to where I could see the tiny settlement lit only by the half moon and a lamp which glowed through a curtain-less window. Homes constructed of the earth with which they sat became larger as I closed the distance, crouched in a defensive pose, rifle sighted at the shack emitting the soft glow.

My men had their own agenda. Keep me safe while moving in to the target: The only lit house in the town. Satellite navigation had pinpointed our location. A ramshackle third-world structure housing three of the enemy who had slain at least six children and as many women in the last forty-eight hours. In a village of only around seventy-five inhabitants, the percentage was huge.

It appeared they were up burning the midnight oil, or perhaps the light acted as a deterrent and the occupants were all sound asleep. It didn't matter. We were going in.

I reached the house first and waited for my men. Viper appeared first and flanked me while the other four motioned to me they'd surround the place. Regardless of how many times I'd forced my way into the center of danger, the adrenalin never waned. It flooded my vital organs, letting me know I stood at the very precipice of life and possible death.

On our typical count of four Viper and I barged in, immediately seeing heat on our night goggles. Two people were in one room with the third in another. We didn't waste time, barreling toward the duo, fingers ready to fire.

Caught unaware, both men stood but didn't

reach for any weapons, knowing they'd be dead before they got close. Raising both their hands, a moment of vulnerability flashed over their faces before their egos closed off any more emotion.

We'd been ordered to kill, but Viper and I liked to draw it out some. Let our targets know death had chosen them. The lives they'd taken mattered to us, and therefore in their honor we played with our prey. We motioned both men to move so that should the other person rise and enter the fray, we'd have him in our sights too. So far, little had been said apart from, "Don't move! Don't move! Get up!" It all happened in seconds. The men probably didn't understand a word we said, but with the motioning of our weapons and the tone of our voices, it proved easy for them to translate our orders.

Viper nodded to me and motioned with his head in their direction. I knew precisely what he meant. We inched closer to the bearded men, who screamed something out in their native tongue. Holding our weapons with one hand we both reached into our holsters and pulled out hand guns, aiming them before dropping our rifles. What we had planned would require closer attention and the rifles were just too cumbersome. My neck ached from the heavy artillery and gear hung over me, but I welcomed the pain. It spurred me on.

"Shut up!" roared Viper.

Movement behind the men brought forth the other occupant, who stupidly raised his gun in our direction behind his cohorts. Before Viper or I fired, the guy dropped to the ground, one of my men appearing in the room. Snake—aka Chris Walker—

stepped over the dead man and switched his aim between each of our targets. We called him snake because of his ability to slither in quietly to awkward situations and take out threats to myself or my team.

He'd get a slap on the back later and praise for his good work. For now though, we were far from through.

Holding position, he waited while Viper and I stepped up to the sons of bitches who'd mercilessly taken the innocent lives of townspeople and probably planned on more carnage. Intel led us to believe they wanted to recruit more soldiers and were doing so without regard to females or minors. We had to put a stop to it.

Placing the barrel of my pistol on one of the men's shoulders I pressed down hard, letting him know I wanted him on his knees before me. Viper did the same. False bravado marked their faces as they spat words about the Almighty.

They had a date with their Almighty soon enough. They'd soon learn there were consequences to their actions even in the afterlife.

Time to have some fun, though. In commanding voices, we ordered them to remove their shirts by lifting the hems of them with the end our guns. We did this until they registered what we wanted. Viper's guy complied but mine continued to spout off at me, so I pressed the barrel between his eyes, watching him sweat. He began removing his shirt. When both men were topless, we barked more orders.

"Undo your belts. Pull your pants down." They

didn't have a clue, so once again we pointed to their scruffy jeans. I chuckled as they decided whether their pathetic lives were worth the humiliation, enjoying their fear. With pants down around their knees, my friend and I looked at each other and laughed. Some of the men in our unit had been known to sport boners during times of extreme stress and actually got off on the rush of terror. These two, however, were limp as fuck. Pitiful really. I wondered if they'd raped any of the women using their poor excuses for dicks.

Lowering my weapon level with my guy's crotch, I loved every moment of his sharp intake of breath and whimper that escaped. I fell to my knees to be on an even keel.

That's right, fucker. You're scared shitless. Welcome to the worlds of all those you've slaughtered.

I gave him my most evil grin.

"What do you reckon, Viper? Should we shoot these assholes in the balls or the heart?"

Viper laughed. "Man, you know me. I'm a sick fuck. I say let's chop off their dicks and stuff them down their throats. Make them choke on it. Then we can put bullet holes in them so they don't die right away. Make it slow and painful."

He was sick. Even more so than me.

Snake stood like a marble statue, waiting for instruction. I couldn't help but wonder if he thought we were insane. Perhaps we were. Perhaps war had created two monsters. I'd analyze it later.

Reaching into my black army boot, I retrieved my knife, sharpened to lethal precision. I twisted it in front of my enemy's face, watching in fascination at his horrified expression.

"You first, man. I want my guy to see what awaits him," Viper offered.

Lowering my blade to a mass of pubic hair, I ran it backward and forward lightly while never losing eye contact with my prey.

He literally began crying with a gun to his temple and his dick about to be removed.

As I brought my hand upward, ready to slice him like a cucumber, a voice called out to me. No, it yelled. A woman. Scared.

The next thing I knew, I dragged in air as I sat upright, not in the dank building in Afghanistan, but in a modern room, light filtering through the half-closed curtains.

Jumping from the bed, I gripped my head, roaring out.

"Harley. Stop. You've had a nightmare. It's okay."

That voice. I could no more ignore it than I could the messed up images from what must have been a crazy dream. It had seemed so real. Spinning, I found her, hovering in the corner of the room. Her frightened eyes killed me. I'd put the fear there. She was afraid of me. Again.

Had I hurt her? Physically?

"Mac…" I moved closer with my hand out, hoping like hell I hadn't added further trauma to her.

Putting her hand out to stop me, she stood taller, drawing on that inner strength I admired so much.

"I'm okay, Harley. More importantly, how are you? Do you want to talk about it?"

Talk about it? Hell no. I couldn't process it, let alone talk about it. I was a monster. I'd tortured someone, even if they deserved it. Not only that, but I'd enjoyed doing it. Jesus. Had I been born a savage or had war done that to me?

Watching Mac take protection in the corner like a frightened bird helped me gain clarity. She was too good for me. I couldn't be what she needed. She couldn't save me. I don't think I can save myself.

Stopping before I reached her, knowing if she reached out to me I'd let her console me, I'd fall into her. I couldn't do that. I couldn't give her any false hope of us being together. Everything had become so fucked up. The beautiful creature before me had the ability to bring me to my knees. I adored her, and yet because of these very real feelings, I wasn't prepared to put her through hell piecing me back together. I would break her.

Taking her in one last time, breathing in her spring garden scent, I held her eyes, trying to convey just how much she held my heart in her hands. I owed her everything and yet I couldn't give her a damn thing without hurting her. She didn't need to save me this time. I needed to save myself.

Dawning lit her eyes. She knew this would be the last time we'd stand here like this.

Tears welled and began their descent down her marred cheeks. Another reminder of what I had brought into her life.

Grabbing my clothes and dressing without saying a word, I couldn't look at her another second and see the pain glaring at me.

Striding out into the hallway, I dragged my heavy feet and heavier heart out her door, feeling like shit for leaving her so vulnerable, but knowing I had no choice.

It was a long walk back to my apartment, but one that would help me cool down. I needed to be alone. Viper would be pissed, but fuck him. Mac was safer with me gone. I didn't even want to go to his place right now. To hear his words would only further my guilt. I craved fresh air and exercise to clear my head. Taking one last look back at her apartment, I steeled myself against the pain in my chest, knowing I'd just broken my own heart.

Chapter Twenty

Mac

I knew he had no intention of coming back. He'd gone. For good. The resignation written on his face and the heartache I'd seen in his eyes told me the truth. He didn't think he was good enough for me. Without me even getting a say. I made it to the bed before my legs gave way. Wretched sobs broke free, threatening to splay my chest wide open. After everything we'd been through, he'd given up. On us. On me.

I didn't have the heart to tell him while he'd been asleep his arm had flung out and caught me on my tender, bruised cheek, causing me to cry out in pain. He'd been too entrenched in memories to waken right away. I'd scrambled away to avoid another swipe, only to find him mumbling garbled words, but flailing his arms. The sheets had been wound around him in an awkward mess, his face scrunched tight.

I don't know what he'd been dreaming of, but it

171

must have been major because it had sent him from my room and my life in the space of a few minutes.

Screaming out, I let loose a string of curses while ignoring my swollen jaw, pounding my fists into the sheets which still smelled of him.

Nothing seemed fair.

Moments later, my doorbell pealed out into the silence. I was tempted to ignore it, but a sliver of hope had me praying it may be Harley coming back to apologize and accept my help. Would he use the doorbell or simply barge in?

Throwing on my robe, knowing I looked like I'd been run over by a truck, I padded to the front door, failing to check the peephole before opening it.

Charlotte stood there looking horrified. As soon as she saw me she threw herself at me.

"Oh my God, Mac! I was so worried. I can't believe you're here."

Her arms squeezed me tightly, causing me to wince. She pulled away. "I'm so sorry. I…"

Scanning my face and injuries and obvious tears, she shut the door and pulled me to the couch.

"Are you okay? What happened? Can I get you anything?"

So happy to see my friend in light of everything, I turned and wrapped my arms around her, bawling uncontrollably.

She patted my back, whispering, "Shh. It's okay now. You're home. I'm here for you."

Thankful to have one person I could rely on, I let her hold me until I felt weak and drained.

Setting me back on the couch she said, "Don't move. I'm getting coffee."

Letting her fuss over me, I wiped at my face, my chest hollow. With Nick gone and now Harley, I needed Char.

When she returned with a steaming mug, I relished it and clung on as if it were a lifeline.

Scratching out a thanks, I asked, "You going in to work this afternoon?"

"Nah. I swapped a shift with Steph at the last minute when I got your message. I'm not due back until tomorrow at six—which means, you're stuck with me for now. I'm taking you out of here for a bit. We can grab you a new cell and eat dinner at a park somewhere."

When I began to open my mouth to refuse, she stopped me.

"It's not up for debate. You're not sitting around here thinking about what happened to you."

Realizing she didn't know about Harley's abrupt departure, I swallowed and began.

"Harley's gone."

"Gone home? Was he here earlier?"

"Yeah, but I mean *gone*, gone. He's not coming back."

Placing her mug on the coffee table, she faced me fully. "What do you mean he's gone for good? That man was out of his mind with worry when you were taken. He moved heaven and earth to get to you. How can he just leave?"

"As cliché as this sounds, I don't think it's me. I think it's him. He's struggling with his memories and has some serious PTSD. He doesn't want to hurt me."

"But he's going to hurt you more by staying

away."

"I know. He doesn't see it that way. We lay down earlier and dozed off. He had a nightmare. Probably about his time at war. He struck out at me unintentionally for the second time. I didn't tell him, but I think he could see my wariness when he woke up."

Shaking her head, and placing her hand on my arm, she offered, "He's an ass if he lets you go. I'm sure he just needs some time to adjust. It must be scary to suddenly have twenty-something years of memories all flooding your brain at once. Not to mention being a hard-core soldier and reliving that shit."

I knew she was right and I should cut him some slack, but she hadn't seen the way he'd looked at me before he left.

Sipping my coffee helped pull me together a little. I didn't feel like going anywhere looking the way I did, but perhaps Char was right. Getting on with things and not moping around might help.

"Oooh, great news too. Word has it we're both getting permanent day shifts." She brightened a lot.

That had me raise my eyebrows. "Permanent? How?"

"There's been two day spots open up. I spoke to Chase and he thinks we're shoe-ins. We've earned it, girl. Quite frankly, I'm over working the graveyard. I need to get a life. Get a man. Speaking of which…that hunk of a friend of Harley's is mighty fine." She flashed me a smile.

Glaring at her, I replied, "Trust me. He's damaged goods too. You don't want to go there."

"I'm not talking long-term. I'm talking about having a little fun. Breaking the dry spell."

I had to hand it to her. She could make me smile, regardless.

Rolling my eyes at her, I scoffed, "Whatever. Good luck with that. He doesn't strike me as being interested in women at the moment."

She swigged her coffee, smiling. "He doesn't realize how charming I can be yet." She batted her lashes in jest, easing the tension in the room.

"I seriously look like crap, Char. If we go anywhere it will have to be where there aren't many people."

"Psssht. Please. Girl, you'd look hot with a bag over your head. But fine, if you're not comfortable heading in to town, we'll grab drive through and take it somewhere. You'll still have to get a cell organized."

I'd been going to anyway, so I'd have to suck it up and venture out. My mood had lifted slightly, so when I finished my coffee I headed to the shower.

***

The phone salesman eyed me with speculation while selling me the latest iPhone, but I held it together. Char stuck close, giving me the courage to not feel like a freak while I filled out the paperwork. She'd managed to apply some makeup and concealer to my face to help, but I knew in all honesty it had done a poor job of hiding what lay beneath. The poor guy probably thought I'd been beaten by an abusive boyfriend.

My stomach rumbled loudly as I signed my name.

"When did you last eat?" Char whispered.

"Ahhh, a sandwich Harley made for me." It hadn't been nearly enough.

"Girl, you're looking gaunt. We need to get you fed, pronto."

And with that we collected my new phone and headed back to Char's SUV and drove to Taco Bell.

"See, that wasn't so bad, was it? Going out in public?" She turned the car into the drive through.

"The salesman couldn't stop looking at me. God knows what he thought."

"Well, you handled it well, regardless."

I didn't answer her. She knew nothing about what had been going on inside me while standing there being ogled like a leper. Normally I didn't worry too much about how I looked, but being every color of the rainbow proved a whole new kettle of fish.

I ended up ordering a seven layer burrito and Char settled on a giant taco.

I didn't do Taco Bell too often, simply because it wasn't on my route home from the hospital. After exhausting days and nights of work, I could never be bothered driving across town for food and just settled for what I happened across on my way home.

As upset as my stomach had been, the food smelled delicious.

We drove to Bandemer Park and sat on the riverfront. Char had been right. Getting out in the fresh air helped. I breathed in and out a few times, letting go of some earlier distress. I prayed Harley would come around after he'd spent a few days getting himself together. Surely the tablets would begin helping soon.

"You're thinking about him, aren't you?" Char asked, ever her observant self.

"I'm trying not to."

"Look. The way I see it is give him some space for now. If you haven't heard from him in a week, call to see how he is. Don't give up on him if you care. You need to show him you're not going anywhere."

"I told him I wanted to be there for him. It's what I do, but he seemed adamant he's doing me a favor. You still think it would be wise to call?"

"It's either that or I'm going over to Viper's house and demand he kick some sense into his friend."

"You just want an excuse to see Viper."

Smiling wickedly at me, she spoke with a mouth full of taco. "Maybe."

I couldn't help but laugh. If Char set her sights on someone or something, she became an unstoppable force. I couldn't wait to see the outcome of this one.

Feeling moderately better sitting in the late sun, chatting about inconsequential stuff, let me relax.

I needed this. Perhaps now that we both were in the running to switch to day shift, we'd get to hang out more. It had been a long while since I'd had a girlfriend outside of work.

"You're smiling," Char commented.

Finishing my mouthful, I nodded. "This is good.

Us. Spending time together just chilling. It's always so frantic at work, we never have time to talk much."

"Yeah well, when you heal up, girl, I'm taking you out. As in a club. At night."

That would be nice too. I'd been so wrapped up in my career that I seriously couldn't remember the last time I went clubbing. Perhaps in my teens.

We spent the better part of the afternoon and early evening sitting at the water's edge, talking. It proved to be one of the best times I've had.

Char dropped me off at my apartment after stopping off for a bottle of wine, which she gave to me and told me to drink.

"It'll help you forget Mr. Hotness."

Like that could ever happen. Unfortunately, sitting alone on my couch with my third glass topped up, I could only think of him. I missed him so much already. In such a short time he'd played a huge role in my life. I felt safe with him around. And he made me feel foreign things I'd hoped we could explore. If he kept pushing me away, that would never happen.

When my head began to swim with the effects of the wine, I turned the television on and immersed myself in *The Notebook*, happy to feel sorry for myself. I didn't want to 'adult' anymore that day. I just wanted to get drunk and wallow.

***

The rest of the week dragged. I wasn't due back at work until Monday when Char and I would begin day shifts permanently. Management had called to confirm after I'd messaged them my new cell number early in the week.

My parents had sent a quick text to say they'd be back home in another week. They were staying with my mother's sister in Dearborn before returning. I couldn't wait to see them and find out all about their holiday. It would be nice to have some moral support besides Char too. I'd no doubt have to confess how my life had nose-dived while they'd been away. It hardly seemed believable, even to me. My dad would probably want to wring Harley's neck for hurting me, but I couldn't blame him. I wanted to wring his neck.

On Saturday, Char was determined to drag my carcass out to a club. My face had healed remarkably well during the week, with a lot of the swelling having eased off. I'd been putting arnica on the bruising, and it had faded to a dim yellow which concealed well under makeup. My eye hadn't fully opened and my jaw still hurt but I was going stir crazy at my apartment.

Harley hadn't called and I hadn't bothered to go visit him. Each day that went on made me believe that he'd been serious about letting me go. My heart hadn't received the memo though, and fluttered every time I thought about him. Which happened a lot. Too much. I couldn't help it. I wondered if he was okay and what he did to occupy his time. I hope he didn't act irrationally and take on another dangerous mission to help him cope. I couldn't imagine the military letting him go anywhere with the state of his mind and his chest wound still healing.

I couldn't bring myself to call like Char had advised. I didn't want another knock-back from him. I didn't want to seem like I pushed or chased him. I just wasn't that type of person.

At eight o'clock sharp, a car pulled up out front and a knock sounded at the door. Checking the peephole confirmed that Char had come for me.

Dressed in my sexiest black dress with three inch heels, I'd tousled my short hair as best I could and applied plenty of concealer and foundation to my face. My lips I'd painted in a cherry red. It felt like I'd gone way over the top but tonight had 'new beginnings' written all over it.

"Holy crap!' Char squealed, embracing me and forcing me to spin around. "I've never seen you look so hot! You're going to have men all over you wearing that."

"Ah, yeah. Not letting drunken hopefuls fawn on me all night. I just needed to dress up a bit to help make myself feel better. After looking like someone's punching bag all week, it's nice to feel half-human again. Plus, I need to get on with things and start over."

"Damn straight you do. Not let's go hit the town!"

Nerves clung to me as we parked and walked a block toward one of the latest clubs to open. Rave was meant to be the hippest club in Ann Arbor, and had been drawing in the crowds for the last month, or so the tabloids had led us to believe.

The queue out the front extended to the end of the block, so we tagged on the end and waited our turn.

Char had dressed in a sexy, low cut white strapless dress that barely covered her backside. I'd never seen this side to her before, but I'd always guessed she had a wild side. After my night of indulgence downing a whole bottle of wine early on in the week, I had no intentions of getting plastered again. It had taken me the better part of the week to gather any energy whatsoever to go out. Not to mention I was still healing.

Her hair was piled high in a messy yet flirty bun. She seemed to be able to pull off the vixen look way better than me. Her eyes were smoked up and popping and I just knew she'd be on the prowl tonight. I could see me driving her car home with or without her later.

It took around half an hour to get to the front of the queue, where a king-sized guy who probably ate steroids for breakfast nodded us both through. We were past the ID stage. I guess working long, stressful hours in a hospital could age you beyond your years.

Walking into the darkened foyer, thumping music shook the walls. A receptionist smiled at us and stamped our wrists.

"Wow, this place is packed!" Char screamed over the pulsating music. Multi-colored lights flashed on and off over the dance floor as bodies writhed and moved in sync to the beat.

"Let's grab a drink and find a table."

Happy to let her lead, I followed, people watching as we walked.

There were two levels, the second one

overlooking the dance floor and seating area. Guys and girls stood holding the railing, watching the lower level, drinking and chatting. Luckily I dressed a tad risqué, as all the females were showing off plenty of skin.

"What do you want to drink?" Char asked.

Sticking to my non-alcoholic plan, I yelled, "Just get me a Coke. I'm still hungover from that bottle of wine you bought me."

Laughing, she ordered for us, grabbing herself a Cosmo and pulling me into the throng of bodies. I wasn't totally comfortable being squished like a sardine, but I kept telling myself to loosen up and just enjoy the night for what it was.

There weren't any tables, so we hung to the side of the dance floor, finding a small clearing where we could stand.

"Are you sure there wasn't somewhere less crowded in town?" I asked, jerking forward when a guy tripped into me.

Turning, he ogled me with red, unfocused eyes. "Oops. Sorry, doll."

Giving him the stink-eye, I waited for Char to reply.

"Yeah, probably, but I wanted to see what all the hype was about. You okay?"

"I'm fine. Just wish there were less people."

"Everywhere is packed on a Saturday night," she replied, swinging her hips to an upbeat tempo.

As I searched the dancers on the floor, a feeling of familiarity washed over me. As if someone I knew hovered nearby. A sensation of being watched. Shivers broke out over my arms and I pulled at my dress a little in an attempt at hiding more. It did nothing but cause me to spill my Coke on the deep red carpet.

Char continued to swing her hips and get further into the groove while I stood awkwardly, my eyes scanning the room for any sign of my unexpected butterflies.

Upon raising my gaze to the upstairs floor, I froze. The room closed in on me even further as I struggled to breathe.

Standing against the railing in the far right hand corner and looking far more delectable than I'd seen him to date was Harley. Beside him stood Viper, whose gaze seemed to be fixated on Charlotte, who had no clue she was under scrutiny. Viper had a serious and pissed off face along with Harley, who clenched the railing so tight, I could almost see his white knuckles. As one of the flashing lights caught his face, it lit up his masculine features, enabling me to witness the masterpiece.

A white collared dress shirt with long sleeves and the two top buttons undone sat atop a pair of fitted black pants. He wore the classy outfit well, and it hit me I'd never seen him dressed up before. He'd always worn Nick's clothes at my apartment, and when I'd seen him last, he'd been in jeans and a tee. He'd look good in anything. I'd seen him in nothing at all and knew what lay beneath. The hard, sinewy physique. Arms to die for, and shoulders wide enough to cover me completely. Shivering, I found it hard to look away and it appeared the same for him.

Just when I wondered if I could summon the

courage to go and say hi, a dark-haired, big-boobed female sidled up to him, placing her hand around his waist. Breaking eye contact with me, he smiled at her and then laughed at something she said. My breathing stopped, my forehead creasing as I squinted to see if I was hallucinating.

Nope. Her other hand came to his chest, remaining there as she stood way too close. His gaze flickered back to me only for a split second before he leant down and said something in her ear which made her laugh. I coughed, spinning away. I couldn't watch. Not for another second. My stomach soured. My mood plummeted. Tapping Char on the arm, I said, "Do you mind if we move?"

"Why? What's going on?"

I really wanted to leave, but seeing my friend enjoying herself, I couldn't do it to her when we'd only just arrived. "Nothing. I just don't like standing here."

Giving me a weird stare, she shoved us around a bit more, pushing people out the way until we stood at the front of the dance floor. It still gave me a view of upstairs.

"Nope. Not right here either."

"What's wrong with you? You look like you've just seen a ghost."

Downing my Coke, I walked off, leaving her calling my name.

"Mac! Wait. Where are you going? What the hell?"

Heading straight for the bar, I opened my purse that I'd hung over my shoulder and pulled out a twenty.

"What can I get you?" the girl behind the bar asked.

"Scotch on the rocks. Make it a double."

My heart thumped in time to the music and my hands were sweaty. What was he doing here? And with a bimbo? He didn't take long to move on. A week, if that.

To hell with him then. If I have to stay at the club longer, I might as well forget about drinking Coke all night and cut loose. Harley looked like he was enjoying himself with the brunette all over him.

Char caught up with me, pulling on my arm. "Please explain, because you're weirding me out here."

"Viper and Harley are here."

Spinning around to scan the crowd, she replied, "They are? Where?"

"Upstairs."

Realization dawning on her face, she nodded. "Oh. We can go if you want."

She'd given me the out I had hoped for, but with my drink in hand, I wasn't going anywhere yet. And besides, he probably hoped I leave. That seeing him with someone else would push me away further. That's what he wanted.

"You know what? No. We're staying. I have every right to be here."

"Atta girl."

Signaling the male bartender to our left with her arm up and a click of her fingers as if she were someone special, he made his way over. Handsome enough. Clean-shaven with a stocky build and buzzed sandy hair. "What can I get you, sweetheart?" he cooed, flashing a cocky smile.

I watched Char flick her auburn hair in a flirty manner. She loved men and seemed to attract them like flies even though she still remained single.

"Another Cosmo, handsome."

Ugh. Maybe I should go. Rotating so my back leaned against the bar, I did some more people watching, waiting on the buzz from my scotch to help me settle. Knowing Harley frolicked upstairs with the well-endowed hooker took up residence in my brain, even though I didn't want it to. I'd come out to forget all about him, but how could I when I felt his very presence nearby?

Char yelled in my ear, causing me to jump. "Watch my drink. I'm going to the ladies'. That first drink has gone right through me."

Acknowledging her with a nod, she left me alone. A rowdy dude stumbled across my path, grinning at me before sidling up to the bar beside me.

"You look like you could use some company."

"Nope. I'm with a friend.

Glancing around, he leered, "I can't see no friend."

"She's in the bathroom and will be back any second."

"Well, I'll keep her spot warm then."

His eyes were bloodshot and pupils dilated.

Turning my back on him, I took another long swig of my drink, hoping he'd go away. No such luck.

"Hey." His hand found my waist as he pulled me

back toward him. "Don't be like that. I could show you a real good time. You and your friend."

Oh hell no. Not happening.

Placing my glass on the bar, I gripped his fingers on my waist and twisted them off, knowing I hurt him, but not giving a damn.

"Ouch. Bitch. What did you do that for?"

"I said no, asshole. What part of that do you not understand?"

Giving him my best death glare, I strode away toward the bathroom, wondering why Char couldn't pee quickly.

After surviving a terrorist abduction, some random drunk dude in a bar would be a piece of cake to handle. Not that I knew how to fight, but my guard would be up for a long time to come when it came to men. Only one had the ability to weaken my defenses and he didn't want me.

When I turned into the alley to the restrooms, I spotted Char. Leaning against the wall facing Viper. They both looked to be in a deep discussion. She probably hadn't even made it to the bathroom.

Viper's body language remained 'standoffish,' but Char overcompensated, leaning in to him and smiling. She liked him. No doubt about it. Not sure if the sentiment was reciprocated, but she'd do her best to make it so.

Not wanting to cramp her style, I about-turned, not really wanting to go back out and face Mr. Handsy either. I took two steps and heard Char call out, "Mac! Look who I found. Come say hi."

My plan of avoiding either soldier was thwarted thanks to my overzealous friend.

Stopping and taking a pause before facing them, I sucked in a deep breath.

Offering Viper a half-smile, I narrowed the gap. "Hey. What are you doing here?" I knew he'd seen me watching Harley earlier, so I didn't pretend to act surprised.

"Same thing you ladies are. Attempting to put the last forty-eight hours behind me." He watched me carefully. "Your face is healing nicely."

"Thanks. Makeup does wonders." Although with the amount of bodies packed into the small club, sweat had probably wiped most of it off.

Did I mention Harley to him? He knew I'd seen him. The way he watched me. Assessing. Curious. Waiting on the words to leave my mouth, Char glanced backward and forward, a slight smirk on her face, knowing me better than I cared to admit. "So. I'm guessing Harley has moved on."

Pushing off from the wall, he moved closer, reaching out to touch my shoulder. "Ah, yeah. About that. Listen, don't take it personally. He didn't come with her. And if I have anything to do with it, he won't be leaving with her. He saw you downstairs and played up to her in an attempt to keep you at a distance. He's seriously pissing me off with his bullshit, but I can't exactly do much about it at the moment. He's my friend and he's been to hell and back. I don't agree with him being a dick to you, and for that I apologize."

"You don't need to apologize. It's not your fault. Any of it."

I really like Viper. He had integrity, loyalty, and respect. Perhaps he would be good for Char, although it would remain to be seen if she could tempt him. So far he hadn't given me any indication that he was interested in her that way.

Only slightly appeased, I nodded, hoping he could eventually talk sense into his friend.

"I, uh, better be getting back." He looked like he wanted to say more, but didn't quite get there and walked off with sympathy in his eyes.

Char seriously stared at his butt, so I stood directly in front of her, cutting off her view and waving my hand in front of her face.

"I wondered where you were. Some random drunk tried to hit on me as soon as you left," I chuffed at her.

"That's because you're hot."

"Ha. Why do I always seem to attract the wrong type?"

"Oh you've attracted the right type, he just can't pull his head out of his ass to give you a chance. I'm going to work on getting Viper to talk some sense into that boy."

"You heard him, Char. He's leaving Harley alone just now. Giving him space to get his head together."

"Yeah, and in the meantime, you're left unable to move on."

Not wanting to have this discussion, I changed the subject. "So what were you and Viper talking about when I arrived? It looked pretty serious."

"Nothing."

"Don't nothing me, Charlotte Newberry. That wasn't *nothing*."

Shifting her eyes multiple times from me to the

space around us, she shrugged. "Just let it go. We were just talking, that's all."

Fine. For now but I'd store it away for another day. Friends didn't hide things and she looked guilty.

"Come on. We came out to enjoy ourselves. Let's forget about men and go dance."

Deciding I needed to immerse myself in the beat, I agreed, letting her lead me back out into the sardine can.

Pushing our way through bodies, I made our spot a gap in the middle. We were practically chest to chest, but proceeded to move in our own unique ways, gradually pushing the people surrounding us back a little.

Unable to help myself, I glanced upstairs and found Viper and Harley in what looked to be a heated discussion. Both men had their arms flailing about. I hoped it wasn't about me, and that Viper had kept his word not to push Harley.

Char must have noticed where my attention was at, because she yelled, "Two of the best looking males I've seen in a long time. Damn, even when angry they look delectable."

I silently agreed with her, refocusing on my own little space, unable to tear my mind away from the image of Harley naked and in my bed, before the abduction.

A hot flush tore through me, causing me to swing my hips with extra gusto and raise my hands above my head in a sultry move.

That man would be the death of me, but for now, I'd just forget about all the crap that had weighed me down of late and enjoy myself.

It didn't take long to get lost in the music. For the first time in ages, I let it carry me away. Sweat dripped down my cleavage but I didn't care. Char and I writhed together and shouted out when a Coldplay song came on.

"We need to do this more often," I yelled.

"Told you. Stick with me and I'll help bring out your wild child."

I didn't doubt that for one second.

Desperately needing a drink to rehydrate, I moved to tell Char, but didn't get very far, A pair of hands latched onto me for the second time. Char's eyes widened, causing me to glance back. Mr. Handsey found me. Shit. The jerk didn't take no for an answer.

"There you are, you little vixen. Thought you could get away that easily?" His bourbon breath wafted around me. It seemed to be leaching from his pores. He'd obviously downed more drinks. If I didn't stand up to him and show him I meant business, he'd never leave. The sensation of his over-zealous hands anywhere near me turned my blood to ice. On instinct, I rammed my elbow back into his gut.

I heard an 'oomph' as he stumbled back. Char grabbed me to move me away, but the guy steadied himself and morphed into pissed off real-quick.

"Oh, you're a real piece of work. You think you're too good for me? You and your slutty friend? I know your type. Dress like whores and then when a man shows interest you act like you didn't dress like that to get noticed." He spat in my face. The last thing I needed was another mental douchebag threatening me.

Char, unable to remain quiet, added her two cents' worth. "Back away, asshole. Clearly my friend isn't interested," she fumed, crouching lower as if ready to throw a punch. After what I'd been through, she wouldn't stand by and watch me get harassed without getting involved. I admired her loyalty. It didn't matter that the guy probably outweighed her by ninety pounds.

Tonight we were two women not to be messed with.

The guy chuckled at my friend's bravado. "A tough bitch, huh? I like that." He swayed and took a step toward Char, momentarily forgetting about me.

She had her stiletto off, aimed at the guy's face. "Take one step closer and I'll remove one of your eyes with my five inch."

The dumb ass must have left his brain at the door, because even with a deadly looking weapon in size seven, he only laughed more. A couple of people beside us glanced sideways and moved out the way, eying the drunk up and shaking their heads. I'd had enough.

Seizing the douche by the arm, I pulled him backward, intending to drag him from the floor, getting him away from Char. The last thing I wanted was a scene. And where were the bouncers when you needed them?

The guy was solid, but not from muscle. He was overweight. Even with his balance compromised with alcohol, I had a job to budge him.

Spinning around to me, he placed both his hands

around me, gripping my ass and burying his head in my neck. God, I nearly fell backward with the weight of him. Finding Char, who was now moving in for the kill with both shoes off, she failed to reach me because Mr. Handsy was dragged away from us by one very fierce-looking Harley. I'd never been more relieved to see him. He had the guy by the throat with one hand, as if he weighed nothing more than a feather, and threw him down onto the ground. The crowd parted but I couldn't see much more, so Char and I shoved forward to find out just what was about to transpire.

"Shit, girl. Are you all right? I could have taken him. These shoes here are my secret weapon." She flashed both shoes before bending down to put them back on.

"I'm fine. I was actually looking forward to seeing where you were going to shove the heels of those things." I attempted to make light of it, even though I felt shaken. What was it with men and me lately?

Viper appeared at Harley's side, looking just as heated and furious.

The two of them together were lethal.

Forcing our way to the front of the growing circle of partygoers, we watched as Harley bent down and punched the guy in his face, blood fanning out from his nose. He then stood up, and with his large, black shoe, he pressed into the neck of the drunk guy, who looked ready to pass out as two bouncers appeared.

"This is better than I could have imagined. That man right there," Char pointed at a savage Harley.

"He just defended your honor. It's obvious he's not over you and cares deeply." She looked smug with herself.

I didn't know what to think. Harley had come to my rescue, not that he needed to because a few seconds later Char would have handled it. Still, my skin warmed over the thought that he'd taken charge. It did mean he still cared.

My gaze traveled up the entire length of Harley. Veins popped where they normally wouldn't. A soldier in civilian clothing—that he was. Blind Freddy could tell he'd been trained in some type of self-defense. He had an air of authority about him now that far surpassed what I'd seen previously. It had only come about since his full memory returned.

His head pivoted, finding me. Or he was seeking me out. I didn't know which. He drank me in, a plethora of emotions written over his face. I couldn't move. Didn't want to. I wanted to drown in him. The pull between us tightened as Viper pulled Harley back so the bouncers could pick up the drunk man and carry him out. The link I needed to sever, in order to save my heart held me in place. Harley took a step toward me, pain leaching from him and flowing into me, but Viper whispered something in his ear and tugged on his arm.

With great restraint, Harley turned and walked away. Again.

Chapter Twenty-One

Harley

If Viper hadn't pulled me back and begged me to give Mac space, I would have lunged for her and held her tight against my chest. Seeing that dick paw her like an animal and not stop when she'd told him to, all but snapped my will.

Standing in the shadows now, watching her friend comfort her, my chest squeezed inward. She looked so fucking stunning tonight, even the woman who'd tried to steal my attention away failed in comparison.

Truth was, as much as I thought of myself as a monster and needed to protect Mac from what I knew I was capable of, I wanted her more than my next breath. Yet how could I ever be worthy of such a woman who saved lives and I stole them? If she knew just what I had done, she'd want no part of my life anyway, so I simply saved her the agony of finding out.

"You did the right thing."

I knew what my friend meant but it didn't make it any easier.

"Did I? She needed me, man, and I walked away. Those eyes. Those freaking eyes. They told me how much she wanted me to go to her. To comfort her. And I didn't."

Groaning, I gripped my head.

"For what it's worth, she will be okay. She has her friend to take care of her. You're trying to get your shit together, bro. For her. You need time."

"Yeah, and what if time pushes her further away? What if she finds someone else?"

"I doubt that. I saw the way you two looked at each other. That doesn't disappear in a hurry."

"You think she'll take me back when I clean myself up? Keep taking my meds?"

Nodding, he placed a hand on my tense shoulder. "Yeah. I do."

I could only hope.

***

The days dragged. A week turned into two and then three. I made no move to contact Mac even though my heart screamed at me to. My meds were beginning to kick in, calming me somewhat. Nightmares still came, but were less prevalent. I actually felt like I could get a handle on life.

Today I was visiting my mother and seeing her for the first time in weeks. Viper had been in contact with her, keeping her updated. Naturally she'd wanted to see me, but I needed to have a clear head first. The meds had given the sensation of brain fog and made the anxiety worse for the first couple of weeks, so I hadn't been good for anyone. After walking out on Mac weeks ago and heading to my apartment, I'd stayed holed up there for a couple of days but knew it was the worst thing for me, so I'd moved temporarily to Viper's where I remained. He'd been nothing short of amazing, making me realize just how much I needed him. He always had my back and I'd always have his. Brothers for life.

My legs jittered up and down as Viper turned into the street of my childhood home. Emotions swamped me as we neared the two story, white cladded home with a porch out the front and garage to the rear. A stone pathway led a trail from the mailbox to the two wooden steps up onto the front verandah.

My dad. Memories flooded back of the two of us out in the garage working on his 1969 Chev Camaro with its bright blue paint and two racing stripes down the front. We spent hours in that damn garage, Dad under the hood and me standing beside him handing him the tools he asked for.

I knew behind the closed door the car would still be sitting pretty. Mom hadn't had the heart to sell it or give it to anyone. It marked too many happy times for her to part with. Just like all Dad's stuff. She'd kept it. Boxed it up but retained it, unable to let go. I understood. If it were Mac...shit.

Don't go there. You saved her, remember?

"You ready?" Viper broke into my thoughts. I hadn't noticed he'd turned off the engine and had his door open.

Not answering, I slowly climbed from his SUV.

The front door opened, stopping me dead.

In the doorway my mother appeared, her hair tied up in a bun, floral sun-dress on, and the beautiful smile on her face I remembered well.

Home. She represented all home was or could ever be. Seeing her face unloaded a ton of emotion through my already amped up psyche. She represented the best parts of me. The young boy who grew up idolizing his father, wanting to be just like him. The kid who had been so shy early on, he hid underneath is mother's long skirts when being introduced to strangers. The youngster who'd spent countless hours sitting on the counter in the kitchen watching his mother bake cookies, licking the bowl clean of the raw dough, and then carrying a basket full next door to old Mrs. James, who would slip me a quarter for being so kind. I could feel the onset of tears. Damn! There weren't many people who could bring me to my knees, but Ma was one of them.

Letting my legs guide me, I powered toward her, picking up speed. I left Viper in my wake, the only thing I needed was the comfort of my mother's arms and her gardenia-scented perfume.

Her arms lifted to welcome me and I couldn't get there fast enough. A swell of tears formed, a whimper leaving my mouth as I reached her and wrapped her up in a fierce hug, never wanting to let go. She felt frailer than I remembered, but I guess she'd been going through a lot of stress in my absence.

"My boy. I've missed you so much."

"Ma." I choked it out, unable to say another word. I sniffed her unique smell, etching it into every crevice of me, regretful that I'd missed so much of her life since I'd joined the military.

Without Dad she lived on her own. It must get awfully lonely.

Pulling back, I drank her in. Her face had aged somewhat, lines deepening around her mouth and eyes. Her hair a little grayer.

"Look at you," she cooed. "My handsome child." Gripping my face in both hands, she planted a kiss on my cheek, her own tears falling like snowflakes.

Yeah, she still thought of me as her baby. I didn't correct her.

"It's so good to see you, Ma. We have a lot to catch up on."

She didn't know about my shooting. About Mac or the abduction. I'd decided to wait to tell her everything in person.

Mom beamed and looked over my shoulder. "Charlie!"

I chuckled at the moniker. She still called him by his birth name, which sounded weird, as everyone I knew called him Viper. Only a handful knew his real name, being a military ghost.

"Hi, Mrs. Harding. Great to see you again." My friend suddenly became younger again also. I could feel his military persona dissolve in my mother's presence. Here we were, just her two boys. Me, her son, and Viper, as close to an adopted child as he could be without actually being one.

"Come in, both of you. I've put the coffee pot on."

Moving inside, I took in the interior, noting nothing had changed. I hadn't really expected it to.

The same beige sofa sat against the main wall that overlooked the large front window. A framed print of the Eiffel Tower sat above it. The smell of coffee wafted through from the kitchen as we followed my mom into the kitchen. It felt strange being home after everything that had transpired. The months since I'd visited seemed like years. Nostalgia filled me as I looked at the wooden dining table set off to the right of the spacious kitchen.

We'd spent many family dinners at that table, discussing our days and working out problems. As strict as my dad had been, he'd also been fair and honorable. A proud man. Proud of his family, he wasn't afraid to praise us to others. His booming laugh drifted across my senses just out of reach and a wave of sadness eased through me.

A hand on my shoulder helped me focus again, my mother watching me with concerned eyes.

"Sit, son. Take a load off."

Pouring three mugs of coffee, she handed us ours and sat opposite in her usual spot. Noting the dark circles under her weary eyes, I worried about her.

"You okay, Ma? You sleeping and eating well?"

I knew she wouldn't tell me if there were something wrong. She had always carried burdens herself, choosing not to worry either Dad or myself.

"I'm fine. Not sleeping well lately, that's all. Don't worry."

I did worry about her living on her own, but I took her word for it.

"So tell me what's been happening with you, Dec?"

Yeah, my mother called me Dec too. It's strange.

With all my faculties back, I knew who I was and yet, I didn't know if I wanted to be him anymore. I liked the man I had been as Harley. I associated the name with Mac. And yet, Dec had been me all along. The person experiencing life thus far.

I glanced over to Viper, who had stopped drinking his coffee to communicate to me with his eyes. They spoke volumes. She didn't need to know most things. If anything.

As if she'd been able to tap into my psyche, she asked the one question I didn't want her to.

"Have you met anyone yet? A nice girl?"

On a cough, I looked back to her, wondering how to answer. Deciding to skim over the details and leave it casual, I replied, "I may have. It's early days yet."

A sparkle gleamed in her eye. She wanted to see me find someone special and perhaps start a family.

"Where did you meet her? You'll have to bring her around for dinner."

Viper cleared his throat too, obviously uncomfortable with where the conversation was headed.

"Like I said, it's early days." How the hell did I explain why I'd met Mac at the hospital?

Saving my ass, Viper spoke up. "She's a friend of mine. I introduced them."

God bless him. He'd lied to my mother, but in this moment, I had to thank him for his quick thinking.

She seemed to buy it, nodding. "Well, I still want to meet her."

Huffing out, I said, "If things progress, I'll bring

her over for dinner. I promise."

We finished our coffees, chatting about nothing in particular, just enjoying the visit. We spoke about our last mission, glossing over a large portion of it. Mothers were on a need to know basis only, and with our ghost status, there was a lot we weren't allowed to reveal. She didn't know the half of it, thank goodness, and it would always remain that way. Her mind still held wonderful memories of my life with her and Dad, and I didn't intend to change it.

"You mind if I go out to the garage?" I asked, needing to feel closer to Dad, even though I could still feel his presence inside.

Mom raised her eyebrows, but nodded. "You sure you're ready? You haven't been out there since your father..." She choked on the last word.

I rose and walked around the table to her, leaning down and burying my face into her neck. "I miss him too."

In fact, I must have grieved for him prior to my shooting, because while sadness still cloaked my heart, it wasn't unbearable.

"You want to join me?" I asked Viper.

Rising, he took the last sip of his coffee and placed his cup in the sink. "Lead the way, brother."

Reaching for the key from a hook on the wall near the sliding door, I headed out. Each step forward pumped blood harder through my veins. It would be like stepping back in time, nothing having changed.

"You ready to do this?" Viper asked from behind me.

"No, but I need to."

Putting the key in the lock on the side door, I opened it, the darkness swamping me for a moment as I reached to the left and fumbled for the light switch.

Even in the middle of the day, virtually no light got in until all the doors were opened.

The smell hit me. Memories followed.

"So, you're getting married, huh?"

Dad leaned over the hood, tightening a hose clamp while I watched. We'd been chatting for the last hour. I relished these times. Our time. Just the two of us on a Sunday morning while Mom cleaned the house.

"Yeah, I guess I am." I smiled down at him. Since telling my parents about marrying Trudy, they'd congratulated me, yet had mixed reactions. My mother had been thrilled. My dad, happy but reserved. I hoped now, he'd talk to me about why he might not be as encouraging as Mom.

"She prepared for the military life? It's not easy, son."

"I've asked her numerous times and explained that I'd be away on missions for weeks at a time, but she supports me and my career. We've known each other since high school, Dad. She knows how much I want this."

"I'm just saying. She might think that now, but when you're away in the middle of a war zone, missing birthdays, holidays, and other special occasions, she might regret her decision."

He lifted his head and looked at me, his face

drawn with worry.

I could imagine how concerned both he and Mom were, let alone having a wife at home, waiting and wondering as well. I'd questioned my reasons for asking Trudy to marry me. Whether I should put her through such anxiety, but at the end of the day, we loved each other, and knowing I had a committed woman back home would keep me going through the darkest of days. I trusted her to stick by me. She'd promised.

"She's strong, Dad. I'm sure everything will be fine." At least I hoped it would. I'd never had any doubts until now.

"And you sure you're ready for marriage? I mean, is she the one?" Obviously seeing my eyes narrow at his probing questions, he cut me off. "Now, I know I sound like I'm not supporting you on this, but marriage isn't easy at the best of times. Throw in a husband who puts his life on the line, it's even tougher. You'll see things, son, that will change you. You won't be the same person you are now. It takes a super strong woman to deal with that."

Breathing out and handing him the wrench when he reached for it, I replied, "I love her. She's been there for me. She can handle it." Couldn't she?

Shit. Dad was putting qualms in my head. What if I got killed in action? She'd be left a war widow. Would she ever get over it?

"You didn't answer my question, Dec. Is she the one? Does she make you a better person? Do you fall asleep at night and wake up each morning thinking of her? Does she help you breathe easier?

Would she put her life on the line for you? Sacrifice it all, like you're doing for her? Does she put those damn butterflies in your stomach, still?"

"Does Mom still do that for you?" I stalled and he knew it.

"You first."

I mean, I did love Trudy. She was gorgeous, sweet, and caring. She looked after me all the time. Our sex life was great.

"Of course. I wouldn't have asked her to marry me otherwise." A niggling little seed of uncertainty grew in my brain that hadn't been there before this conversation. My dad meant well and I knew he spoke from experience but, shit. I didn't need to be having reservations. I had to steer the discussion in another direction. "Now you answer the question."

Dad straightened from under the hood and faced me, a wistful expression on his face. "Son, I knew your mother would end up my wife for life the day I saw her, picking flowers in her parents' front garden as I rode home from my after school job. I nearly ran off the road and into a parked car. She took my breath away. As I passed, she turned to me and smiled. I swear the sun shone even brighter in that moment. My heart expanded. Nothing has changed to this day. She still lights up the room when I walk in. I still find myself catching my breath when she smiles."

Shaking off his lucid reverie, he moved to the work bench to grab a rag, wiping his hands on it.

"I just want you to experience that, son. 'Cause I'm telling you, when you find it, you'll know."

He didn't speak any more about my marriage.

He'd said what he needed to. After that, he'd grabbed a beer out of the small fridge and we'd sat on two crates in the garage, in quiet contemplation.

"You have another memory? Man, you look like you've seen a ghost."

Letting my eyes adjust, I turned to Viper, half-expecting to see my father, but finding my worried friend instead.

"Yep. Just shooting the breeze with my old man in this very garage."

"Well, that's twice today I've seen you shed tears."

"What?"

"Dude, you're crying."

Lifting my hand to my eyes, I found them wet again. Christ! I never cried. The memory had felt so damn real. All it had taken was a visit to my parents' house and a lucid memory of my dad. I guess visiting had affected me more than I thought it would.

Attempting to shake it off, I spun and eyed the very car I'd just been daydreaming about. She stood sleek and proud, exactly the way Dad had left her. My fingers reached out to touch the paint, fragments of my memory lingering as I walked around her to the driver's side. Opening the door, I sat behind the wheel, failing at keeping the tears at bay. It was all too much. The emotion. The loss. I'd never get to share this space with my father ever again. Never hear his advice born out of love. Share a beer or two or take her for a drive after fine-tuning the engine.

I let my hand travel to the glove compartment, flicking the button to open it. Focusing on the interior and its contents, my eyes landed on Dad's favorite pair of aviator shades, sitting atop the original owner's manual. Picking them up, my gut overturned and my shoulders sagged as incredible grief swamped me further. I couldn't keep in my wretched sobs as I broke down. Not even at the funeral had I let go because I'd been determined to stay strong for Mom.

Now in the quiet and solitude of Dad's favorite possession, his passing came crashing down and there wasn't a thing I could do to stop it. Twelve months of locked away anger at him being taken so soon. Twelve months of still expecting to see him or hear from him. Twelve months of wondering if there was anything we could have done to avoid his heart attack. Not being with him before he died. All of it compounded and crashed into me.

I barely heard the passenger door open and close as Viper got in. A hand went to my shoulder and squeezed, but no words were uttered as he let me mourn.

My body weighed a ton under the burden of sorrow.

Like a shark, it tore strips off me, letting me bleed out with no mercy. I sat crying like a girl for ages, Viper at my side as always. I'm surprised he hadn't shot out a sarcastic remark to lighten the mood, but then, he'd always known when to keep his mouth shut. I don't know what I would have done without him over the years and I was glad he shared this moment with me.

Feeling the last of my heaving gasps ease, I placed the sunglasses back in the glove compartment where they belonged and closed it, not knowing what the hell to do from here.

"You want to go grab a beer? A final goodbye to your dad?" Viper quietly asked.

Nodding, we got out. I pulled myself together enough to hopefully hide my breakdown from Mom and went to take a step toward the door when I halted. My mother was already inside, tears in her own eyes. She'd heard everything.

Stalking to her, I wrenched her small body into mine, squeezing her tightly, letting her shed her own grief over mine.

"He was so proud of you," she whispered.

Hearing it made me grip her even harder. "I know, Ma. I know."

I couldn't imagine what she'd been through and how she managed to continue on so well. They'd been perfect together, complementing each other so well, it just didn't seem fair that fate had stepped in.

Gathering herself and pushing off me, she lifted her hand. Dangling from her fingers were a set of keys I instantly recognized.

"He wanted you to have the car. I wanted to make sure you were ready before I handed the keys over. I think you are now." She smiled warmly, her wet cheeks crinkling.

Overcome with shock and delight that she was gifting me with something Dad had treasured, knowing I too would look after it, I gently took the keys from her.

"Are you sure? I have nowhere to store her."

"I'm positive, and you can keep her here and drive her whenever you wish."

Wow. I truly didn't have any words other than, "Thank you."

"You can keep her at my place if you want, bro. I've got a double lock-up garage. It's up to you."

Glancing at my mother and then at Viper, I digressed. On one hand it would be great having it at Viper's house because his place was closer to mine. And on the other hand, every time I wanted to drive it, I could visit Mom if it remained here. Tracing her bloodshot eyes and tear-stained face with my fingers, I knew my answer.

"Nah, man. Thanks for the offer, but I'm going to leave her here."

My mother's eyes lit up. She knew why I'd refused my friend over her. Giving my hand a squeeze, she began to walk away, calling over her shoulder, "Take her for a spin."

I planned on it and I knew just where I wanted to take her. Checking the time on my watch, I smiled.

"Can I take a raincheck on that beer, bro?"

Chapter Twenty-Two

Mac

With my face back to normal and my permanent day shift in full-swing, life had resumed some sort of routine. I'd switched from ICU to the Emergency ward and had been run off my feet all morning with a head-trauma victim, a teen with broken ribs and fractured pelvis from a motorbike accident, and a child with a fish hook in his finger.

It was great having Char in the ward with me. Although she had her own patients to tend to, we'd caught five minutes in between casualties to catch a breather and chat.

My feet ached and fatigue gripped me, all before three o'clock in the afternoon. My sleep had dwindled to just a few hours a night at best since Harley had gone. I still thought of him, wondering how he coped. I couldn't help it. The nurse in me would never leave. Plus, I still cared about him. Really cared. I missed him a lot and wished he would make contact. I hadn't called Viper to ask, giving Harley the space he requested.

Nick, my ex-boyfriend, hadn't made contact either, which didn't bother me. I knew it was over long before he packed up all his belongings.

Still, with no male presence around, it had been lonely. Char had done her best to help me move on, taking me out and attempting to hook me up with male nurses or doctors, but I turned her down each time. The only man I kept picturing had endless dark brown eyes that captured me every time. A tipped up mouth soft enough to eat, and molded arms strong enough to hold me through the night.

"Earth to Mac. You zoning out again?"

"Just thinking."

"About Harley?"

"I…uh…" She could read me well enough to tell if I lied, so I opted for the truth. "Is it that obvious?"

"Girl, you've been off your game for weeks. I see that faraway look you get in your eyes when you think no one's watching. It's not a, 'I have been to hell and back' look either, it's more of a 'I miss him so damn much' kind of expression."

Laughing at her precise observation, I checked my watch, knowing I needed to get back to work. "Yeah ,well, it's obvious he's got no intention of making contact, so I need to forget about him and get on with things. I've been trying. It's just hard, you know?"

"Yeah, I do. You really liked the guy. Give yourself more time. I'm sure in another month or so you'll be asking, "Harley who?"

Hmmm. I couldn't be so sure, but I did need to focus on my work for a change. It wasn't healthy to obsess over something I couldn't have.

Placing one foot in front of the other, I left the break room and headed back to the nurses' station. When I rounded the corner, and saw who stood at the desk, all breath left me. My legs weakened and I had to place a hand on the wall to steady myself.

Leaning with his back to the reception area, with his arms folded, wearing a leather jacket and dark blue jeans with his black work boots, he looked every bit as good as my memory served.

Better even. His hair had grown slightly longer, his face clean-shaven. Even in profile, he oozed authority and presence.

I stood and gaped, letting myself take him all in, wondering why he had come.

Did I quietly walk away or did I go to him and ask what he wanted?

I didn't have to wait to decide. He made the decision for me, turning and zeroing in on me with all the intensity of a starved man during a famine.

My body wouldn't move. I should have walked away. The rational part of me screamed to go back the way I had come but with his utmost focus on only me, I just couldn't do it.

People moved all around us but they were nothing more than abstract shapes as I took in all his gloriousness. He appeared less angry and more in control. Calmer.

I stood still to see what he'd do, not wanting to go to him, but not wanting to move. His lips lifted slightly as he took the first step. He hadn't looked away and neither had I. I didn't want to miss a thing. The last three weeks had been torture. I thought I'd never see him again. Especially not in my place of work. Speaking of which, how did he get into the Emergency Ward?

As he neared, my breathing changed, almost coming to a complete stop. His essence reached out to touch me, wrapping its tentacles around me. His scent came next, coating my nostrils, sparking a hormonal reaction. My body sold out my rationality. Traitor.

He filled the space in front of me until my eyes leveled with his neck. He swallowed hard, the tight muscles bulging with the effort, as if he too struggled to remain composed.

"Angel."

His name for me. He hadn't called me Mac. Did that mean...? No. It didn't mean a thing. Old habit.

"What are you doing here?" I attempted to keep the hope out of my voice as I finally looked up and into his absorbing stare.

"Waiting for you to finish."

"What? Why? I don't finish for another two and a half hours."

"I'll wait."

"But you can't just hang around in here. As you can see..." I swept my hand around us. "We're busy. Speaking of which, I need to get back to work."

Knowing I still had rounds to do, I moved to shuffle past him, unable to soak in his beauty any longer. I sucked in a sharp breath when his large hand seized my arm. Not hard, but with enough pressure to let me know he needed to tell me something.

"Wait. Please. We need to talk."

Not sure what he wanted, I didn't want to make things easy for him. He'd pushed me away when I needed him and now he just waltzed in here expecting me to concede to his request.

"How did you get in here, anyway?"

Looking away for a second, he focused again. "I have my ways."

"Of course you do. You have military clearance, right?" It came out a little snarkier than I intended.

"Look. I'll stay here all Goddamn night if I need to, but I'm not leaving until we've talked."

Hearing my name paged, I had no choice but to agree. I didn't have time to stand and tell him all the reasons why talking would be a bad idea.

"Fine. Stay out of the way and don't interrupt me again while I'm working." I didn't wait for an answer. I took off to the room I'd been called to, happy for some breathing space, yet nervous about being alone with him. Had he come to tell me he was shutting me out completely? That he'd decided to work things out with Trudy after all?

Gah! Now my brain ran at the speed of sound, overthinking everything. Damn him showing up. I had been on the cusp of accepting his decision to shut me out and move on. Now, after seeing him again, I clung to the slight possibility that maybe, just maybe he'd want to work things out. It didn't bode well for the rest of my shift.

Chapter Twenty-Three

Harley

I knew she'd arrived before I turned and saw her stunning face. My body came alive and all my senses were on high alert. I gave her a moment before I focused everything I had on her. I'd be the last person she expected to see at her work. Especially in the area reserved for emergencies only. I was hardly that, although the favor I'd called in from her friend Charlotte had paid off handsomely. At first she'd given me an earful about what an asshole I'd been, but after explaining why I needed to see Mac and what my intentions were, she'd conceded, albeit, begrudgingly.

So here I stood, the slow pivot of my legs bringing me in line with my lifeline. My breathing apparatus. The gorgeous woman who'd unwittingly burrowed into the thick walls of my heart and found me when I'd been lost. The weeks that had passed and the medication helping me settle, had brought about a new clarity. Life sucked without Mac in it.

215

She shined light in the darkness. I wanted what she had to offer. I never should have pushed her away, but I didn't know any other way. I still didn't know if I'd hurt her, but with each day, my resolve strengthened. I needed to fight for the good. What had transpired in my past needed to stay there and not own me. It would be a new kind of battle I'd be fighting for years to come but for Mac, I'd try. I owed her that. If she still wanted me. I couldn't blame her if she hated me and didn't want anything to do with me.

Her gaze, when I found it, told me all I needed to know. Mixed with the initial shock of my appearance, like some ghost from the dark, I saw a flicker of hope. That little spark was all I needed. My feet moved before my brain could catch up. Her pull led me.

Christ, she epitomized the perfect woman in her scrubs, and I wanted nothing more than to push her up against the wall and take that mouth. Oh, how I'd missed that mouth. It tried to smile but didn't quite get there, and I knew I shouldn't expect her quick forgiveness, but damn, if I didn't want to see the way it upturned and dimpled when she showed me her pearly whites.

Mixed amongst the sliver of hope I could see anger. Perfectly justified. Surprised she hadn't shunned me completely, I noted the way she shone under the fluorescent lights as if otherworldly.

"Angel." My angel. I needed her alone to plead my case but I knew it wouldn't happen at her place of employment.

Asking what I was doing here, I explained I was

waiting for her to finish.

She appeared to put her shutters back up again, straightening her spine. When she agreed to talk after her shift, my shoulders and anxiety eased somewhat. I'd hang out in a hard chair if I had to, but I wasn't leaving without her.

Watching her walk off after she'd been paged, I followed the sway of her hips, hoping like hell I'd get to feel them beneath me again. I had some serious groveling to do, something which I had never needed to do before. If that's what it took, I'd do it. I'd kiss the ground she walked on.

When she'd asked me how I'd come to be in the Emergency section, I'd dodged giving her a proper answer. I wouldn't sell her friend out. I'd promised.

With chaos unfolding around me, I slid into my own head, filling my time with images and thoughts of Mac. From the moment I'd found consciousness after the shooting, it had been her. Only her. And I'd all but blown it with my own selfishness.

To think of all she'd been through since knowing me. The demise of her relationship with Nick, which in all fairness had already begun to crumble before I appeared on the scene but still, maybe they could have worked it out.

Her apartment being ransacked. The abduction and beatings, feeling like she would die in that dank, warehouse. And to top it all off, I'd been a total ass and set her aside as if she were nothing more than a passing thought.

Through it all, she'd survived. The way her demeanor had shifted into that of a battle-hardened woman had raised my respect for her even more.

She had returned to work to continue her destiny of helping others, even when she'd needed help herself. That's the type of woman I wanted. One who would carry me to my own salvation.

Chapter Twenty-Four

Mac

"Hello? Nurse? I asked for an update on Brock Henderson in room five. Have we got his bloods back from the lab yet?"

Snapping out of a head full of Harley, I answered swiftly, "Sorry, doctor. I'll get on it."

Scurrying down the hallway toward room five, where seven-year-old Brock had been brought in with a high fever and rash, I mentally berated myself for letting my work suffer.

I'd been standing with the boy's file in my hand at reception when Dr. Bennett had caught me. Feeling like an idiot, I pushed the curtain aside to assess Brock, his worried parents hovering.

"Any news yet, Nurse?"

"I'm sorry. I'm going to check the computer now to see if they've sent the results. Shouldn't take too long." Unless I lost my mind to one hot, thick-headed soldier again. Not happening while I was on the clock.

219

Each holding bay had a computer for easy access to information. I checked to see if the bloods were back, glad to see they'd been sent through.

Scanning the screen, I couldn't find any obvious signs of the youngster's illness. Full blood count—normal. Kidney and liver function—normal. Nothing stood out in red. A good sign but frustrating for the parents, who wanted answers.

"Everything appears fine. I'm sure it's just a virus. We'll keep him here a little longer until his fever comes down. Kids often get a rash with a viral infection so we need to make sure he gets plenty of fluids and rest to help fight it." I smiled. I'd pressed down on the rash earlier, making sure it paled upon depression, which it had, or I may have ordered more tests to discount meningitis. I'd witnessed rashes associated with meningitis and this one differed. It was blotchy and only appeared on his front torso. More like a heat rash. The boy appeared coherent. I wasn't ready to put him through the trauma of a spinal tap.

Both parents appeared pleased with the results, nodding at my diagnosis.

Leaving them with the promise of my return shortly, I redrew the curtain, almost bumping into Char, who hurried down the central aisle.

"Wow, girl. Slow down." I steadied us both as we collided.

"Hey! Sorry. Got a head trauma victim just brought in. You free?"

Checking my watch, I nodded. "I've got a few minutes spare."

We both headed to the ambulance entrance. I

was grateful to be distracted enough to let Harley out of my thoughts for a while.

***

When my shift ended, I clocked out and wandered around my ward, wondering if Harley had ended up waiting or got tired and left.

I did a quick walk around, finding him in a waiting area off to the side of the hallway leading to the short stay ward. He stood as soon as he saw me. I'd changed out of my scrubs into a pair of jeans and a long sleeved blue shirt with my Converse sneakers.

He looked me over slowly, eliciting a series of shockwaves in his aftermath, but I tried not to show it.

"You ready?" he asked in a dry voice.

"Yep. I'll follow you."

Shaking his head, he moved in closer. "I'll bring you back to pick up your car. I want to take you for a ride."

"Oh. Okay. Let's go then."

Not sure where he wanted to take me, I walked alongside him, trying not to sneak peeks every few seconds. His presence disarmed me. I felt him all the way to my toes, and I wasn't sure how I would get through the next couple of hours.

We left through the main entrance, moving across the parking lot. The sun still shone at 6 p.m., a gentle breeze wafting over us. We hadn't uttered a word, and I found it a little disconcerting, considering we'd never had an issue with conversation before.

After a couple of minutes, Harley stopped before a 1969 Chev Camaro. I didn't consider myself a car buff, but I liked a classic. My Mustang proved that. For a moment, I ogled the fine machine, appreciating the gleaming blue paintwork and sleek lines.

Whistling, I crooned, "Oh my God. She's gorgeous!" Looking up to Harley with a bright smile, I almost skipped closer. "She yours?"

"Yup. She is now. My mother gave her to me today. Ah…she belonged to my dad."

Knowing his father had passed, I stopped short of the passenger side door, looking over to him. He wore a wistful expression so I kept the mood light, not wanting to bring about any pain.

"Wow! She's in fine condition. Not a scratch on her. You sure you should be driving her?"

"I'm keeping her at Mom's, but I wanted to take her for a spin."

"You've seen your mom?" It wasn't so much a question as a statement.

"Yeah. I went around today." He looked away as he spoke.

"How did she react to everything that's happened?" I imagined she would be shocked and hurt over Harley's shooting and his temporary amnesia.

"Ahh, I didn't tell her."

I spun further to face him. "You didn't tell your mother you were shot?"

He looked at me then, his darkened eyes filled with indecision. "I didn't want to worry her." His voice had softened. I could see how much he loved his mom.

"Still, she deserves to know."

He stared into me, nodding minutely, his mouth set.

Eager to get in and see how she rode, I waited for Harley to insert the key to unlock her. No automatic locking on this baby.

When he brushed against me, a light tremor had me shivering. I should be getting into my own car and going home, not taking a drive in a confined space with a man who had recently tried to break me and now still had the power to turn me into a puddle of desire.

Waiting on him to move, I quickly climbed in and closed the door, breathing in the 'olden day' smell. Everything inside had been restored, from the upholstery to the steering wheel and dashboard. I was impressed.

Harley moved to the driver's side and got in and absorbed even more of the space we needed between us. His leather jacket crinkled as he got comfortable and inserted the key into the ignition. I appreciated the low rumble as the engine fired up, excitement bubbling over.

His face lit with as much amusement as mine, our shared love of cars momentarily bridging the gap that had threatened to tear us apart.

Turning his head to mine, he smiled. "Hang on, angel."

Easing out of the parking lot and onto the street, he hit the gas, propelling us forward. I gripped the seatbelt, enjoying the power the car yielded.

She was a smooth ride and her engine ticked over without missing a beat. There had been a lot of love poured into her, I could tell. Glancing at Harley, I noticed the half-smile on his face as he maneuvered her in and out of traffic.

Unaware of where we were headed, it wasn't until we turned into the familiar apartment complex that I realized he'd driven to his place.

My nerves ratcheted up a notch at being in his space. It seemed an incredibly personal place to be having 'the talk,' but there wasn't much I could do about it. We were here now. I'd need to suck it up and deal.

He pulled into a visitor park at the end of his row of apartments. Having only one garage space, I knew his truck would be locked up inside.

Before I could get out, Harley was around to my side, opening the door for me. Chivalry wasn't dead after all. Either that or he was pulling out all the stops.

We still hadn't spoken much, if at all, and I felt a little lost.

Following him into the apartment, I let him lead me into the small living room.

"You want a coffee? Wine? Beer?" He removed his jacket and threw it over the arm of the sofa, gifting me the view of his sculpted arms. Hell, I loved a nice set of arms.

Needing something to help ease my nerves, I replied, "Wine would be good. Thanks."

The apartment smelt of Harley. His aftershave and whatever else made up his unique scent.

A truck picture, similar to the one he'd given me

an orgasm against, hung on the wall opposite. I recalled Trudy walking in on us. Aside from that embarrassing moment, it had been so hot. If she hadn't arrived, I knew we would have ended up in Harley's bed. I wouldn't have stopped him.

Recalling the sex at my place, I'd never experienced such a heated connection with a man. Perhaps comparing him to Nick wasn't a great gauge, but I hadn't been with that many guys beforehand. The way Harley had looked at me with reverence and touched me in equal measure hadn't been just about sex. It had been way more. At least for me.

"Penny for your thoughts?" The deep, scratchy voice dragged me out of my daydream.

He held out a glass of red wine, which I eagerly took. "Thanks."

No need to explain where my mind had been.

Sitting down beside me, he took a sip of the beer he held before placing it on the table. Running a hand over his face and up into his hair, he cleared his throat.

"I owe you an apology."

Knowing he did, I still acted dumb. "Oh?" I held onto the wine glass like a lifeline.

"I don't expect you to forgive me for the way I acted. Pushing you away. I was scared. Scared of everything that came crashing back to me like a freight train. Since you met me, I've brought nothing but stress and pain into your life. I didn't want to do that anymore." He reached for his beer, taking another long pull.

I didn't say a word. He needed to purge his

feelings.

Breathing out hard, he continued, finally turning to me, capturing me with his sexy eyes. "I owe you everything. Everything. My life. If not for you when I woke up, and the way you took me into your home, I might not even be sitting here. I treated you like shit and I'm sorry. I didn't want to push you away, but I didn't want to keep you close and hurt you, either."

His eyes reached into me with their intensity, allowing me to see the truth. His sadness and pain.

It mirrored my own. My heart bled for him. I hated seeing him carry the burden of war and death. No man should have to.

In a meek voice, I asked, "What changed?"

Reaching out tentatively, he cupped my cheek. The warmth from his fingers made me shiver against the coolness of my wineglass. Momentarily closing my eyes, I savored the feel of his touch, not realizing how much I needed it.

"You. Not having you around. I missed you like crazy. Call me selfish, but I can't stay away. I don't want to. The medication has helped. I'm not having nightmares as much and don't feel the incredible anger I did the last time you saw me. I feel…okay. Angel."

His eyes pleaded with me to understand while his thumb brushed backward and forward over my cheek.

"I don't want to lose you. You're the best thing that's ever happened to me. Please! Do you think you can forgive me? Do I have any chance to make things right?"

Not wanting to let go of this moment, I studied him some more. The way his lips glistened and his cheeks had hollowed out slightly. The line between his brows, which appeared more pronounced since we'd seen each other. His heavy lashes jutting out from turbulent eyes, which had darkened under my perusal. The air of authority he'd carried in the hospital had waned somewhat, allowing me to see the true man. Declan or Harley? Who was he? I needed to know before stepping forward into the unknown.

"So, now that you have your full memory back, are you Declan or Harley? What do I call you?"

I truly didn't know Declan. I'd only experienced the angry snippets he'd shown me. Harley had been a clean slate.

"To be honest, I'm hoping you will accept me as Declan. It's who I am and who I've always been. I need to accept that person, flaws and all. I guess I wanted to stay Harley because I associated him with you. He didn't have horrific memories of war and all the other shit that's happened in my life, but I can't run away from it all now. It's up here." He tapped his forehead. "The big question is, do you want me the way I am now?"

He'd always be Harley to me. It's all I've known. Could I accept the rest of him? Flaws and all? As strange as it would be, I needed all of him. Not just pieces. I wanted to know everything.

Placing my hand over his, which still rested on my cheek, I slowly nodded.

"Whatever your name is, it doesn't matter to me. It's who you are in here." My fingers pressed against his heart. "The man I first met wasn't someone different. He simply didn't have the weight of his memories to deal with. You've been Declan all along, you just didn't know it."

He smiled. Truly smiled for the first time, and it lit him from the inside out.

Gripping the back of my neck, he pulled me in almost touching. God, he smelled good. I truly wanted to stay mad at him, but I just couldn't. He'd been in a dark place and I could understand him trying to protect me. Perhaps I'd do the same. All that mattered was he felt better and had brought me here to apologize. I'd been miserable without him. If he was prepared to try, then so was I.

"Do you have any idea how incredible you are?" He groaned.

"Show me," I whispered, unable to wait any longer. I mashed my mouth against his, forcing him to open as I delved my tongue inside, tasting him. Tingles shot through me as his tongue played lightly with mine, his shapely lips devouring me, the drought officially over.

Gripping each side of his head, I held him firm while I took my fill. It only sufficed to mildly allay my need, and he must have felt the same because two big hands came under my armpits, lifting me so that I sat astride his lap. Pressing myself into him, he gripped my denim-clad ass and dragged me harder against his groin. Desperation overtook me. I needed him everywhere. What we had wasn't enough.

Tearing my mouth away, I gazed into his heavily dilated eyes. He appeared drunk like me. Drunk on each other. "Take me to bed. Now," I ordered.

A lazy grin lifted his cheeks. "You bossing me around?"

"Yes. Don't talk. Just do it."

Smacking his lips back to mine with a satisfied gleam in his eyes, he stood, taking me with him. I shackled myself to his heavy thighs, letting him carry me to his room. I didn't take any notice of anything other than his chest rising and falling heavily and the solid beat of the pulse in his neck. Hitting the edge of the bed, he fell and I went with him, landing in a mess of limbs on a pair of black satin sheets. I stared at them only long enough to wonder if he'd put them on the bed, knowing he'd be bringing me here before my head was turned to fuse our mouths together again.

We both groaned as we writhed on the bed, needing to shed our clothes.

Gripping his shirt, I broke our contact and fumbled with it beneath me, attempting to pull it up and over his head. Arching his back, I managed to rid him of it in a less than graceful manner, the sight before me, stealing my breath. His broad shoulders appeared more buff, veins running a path down his arms to his hands.

"Someone's been working out," I breathed.

"Keeps me focused," he replied. "Do you want me, angel? All of me? No going back. This is it. You're all in or you're all out. Good and bad."

Not having to second-guess myself, I shot back, "Yes. I'm in. One hundred percent. Now stop talking with that fine mouth and put it to better use," I teased.

He chuckled. "Let's get naked first and I'll show you just what my mouth can do."

Flipping me so I lay beneath him, he took his time removing my clothes, his hands, eyes, and mouth worshipping each inch of skin he bared.

I'd never felt more wanted. This messed up, desirable man who had sacrificed himself to save me. I'd never forget it and do everything in my power to help him heal.

When the last shred of clothing was thrown on the floor, our bodies connected like two magnets. I fit into his massive frame perfectly as he wrapped me up in his arms, protectively. His kisses had me high like an addict, an addiction I never wanted to quit.

His hard mass jerked beneath my pelvis, so I rubbed harder into him, getting the reaction I hoped for. Throwing his head upward for a moment, he brought it back down to face me, eyes like blazing sin, teeth gritted as he hissed in his pleasure.

Both my hands moved down his body, tracing every dip and valley as they settled on his perfectly round ass.

"Is this what you want, Mac? Is this what you need?" He flexed beneath my grip, bringing friction just where I needed it.

Showing him my assent with a simple nod, he lowered his mouth to my aching breasts, nipping and sucking while gently pulling my thighs further apart beneath him.

I gasped as his teeth grazed my nipple a little too hard but he soothed it with his tongue.

"Are you clean?" he asked, taking me by

surprise.

"Yes. I haven't been with many men. You?" I guess we needed to get it out of the way because he'd made no move to reach for a condom. I didn't want him too. I needed to feel him bare inside me. I took birth control pills every day, so there was no issue of me getting pregnant. Come to think of it, we hadn't used a condom the first time. A little late for the question now.

"I get tested regularly in my job, but I've always used a rubber." Licking his already moist lips, he drilled into me with his eyes. "We good to go? You ready?"

"Just do it," I practically begged, gripping his butt further, lining him up.

Without further ado, he speared into me, a garbled noise escaping from my throat at the sheer relief and ecstasy of him touching me in places long forgotten. Hovering over me on his forearms, he lavished me with a stare so intense and filled with love, I became spellbound.

He paused, fully seated in me, the only sound our harsh breathing. "Do you see me?" he asked.

For a moment, I didn't know what he meant, but as I drowned in the emotions he showed me, having let his wall of hurt disappear so that only the man I'd come to fall for remained, realization dawned.

"I see you. All of you."

Kissing me fiercely, he reared back and powered back into me. Once. Twice. Three times before stopping again.

"I see you too. My fucking angel."

His words sealed every crack that had been

widening. Filled every lonely space present for so long. Held me captive as he rolled us to our sides and lifted my leg high up his thigh before his hand softly stroked my neck, shoulder, and then breast.

His fight for redemption strengthened my resolve to assist him in becoming whole again. Feeling his gentle touch and watching the way he gave me more of his true self, I knew in that sensational moment my heart belonged to him. He'd stolen it without even knowing it.

"I love you." Truth be damned. If he didn't want to hear it, then so be it.

Lifting his head off the pillow and bringing his face closer to mine, his eyes widened.

Unable to breathe until he reacted, I waited.

"What did you say?"

"I love you. I understand if you—"

He cut me off with a kiss from heaven. Slow and languid, deepening to the point of almost tipping me over the cliff of pleasure, but not quite. I teetered so close and he hadn't needed to do much. He hardened inside me further, driving me crazy.

Sucking on my bottom lip, he brushed his mouth across my cheek, resting it on my ear. "I am so in love with you, angel. You have no idea. From the moment I heard you singing while I remained in a coma, you had me."

Elated to hear him admit his feelings, knowing they reciprocated mine, I grinned madly.

"Now. I don't know about you, but I'm ready to heat things up a bit. On your knees, angel."

His commanding voice returned, along with an undercurrent of his wild side. Not wasting any time,

I pushed from under him and positioned myself in the center of the bed, watching him, proud and strong, climb off. Expecting him to kneel on the bed, he gripped my legs and pulled me down to the edge, instead.

"Face flat, Mac. Show me that stunning ass high in the air."

Vulnerable but not the least bit bothered by it, I complied, feeling his hands run over my butt cheeks in soothing circles.

"Such a fine sight," he murmured.

Fisting the black sheets, knowing he'd passed the point of slow and sensual, I braced for impact.

Crying out from the new angle and the entire length of him drilling into me in one go, I let myself go fully, embracing his size and strength.

He roared out as he hit my cervix, a flurry of delicious nerves coming to life inside me as my walls contracted around him.

"Jesus, Mac. Do that again."

I squeezed him using my muscles, loving the noise it dragged from him.

Withdrawing almost completely, he drove in again and again, his grip firm on my hips as he ran his own race. I hung on for the ride, happy to be taken shamelessly.

"Yesss. So good." I moaned every time he bottomed out.

His deep continued stroking swept me along on a wave of pleasure. The raw brutality of it had me in my element. The part of me I'd been searching for. The hunger. The passion. I had it. Finally.

Climbing up onto the bed, Harley—I'd still

always think of him as Harley—shrouded me with his body, one hand coming around to cup my breast while his mouth sucked and licked my back as he continued to pound into me.

"Fuck, angel. I could do this all night. You feel phenomenal."

So did he, but I couldn't speak because just as I went to open my mouth, the wave I'd been riding crested, spiraling me into a vortex of such intense pleasure my vision wavered. The room spun and my knees gave out, but I didn't fall.

"I got you." Big hands lifted me back up, holding me against him as I convulsed. He paused after each thrust, holding deeply to extend my pleasure until I became too wrung out to move.

I resembled jelly.

Harley grunted, increasing his pace until with an almighty shudder and four jerky thrusts, he growled out his release. Filling me. Claiming me.

Collapsing on top of me, we both fell forward. Sweat coated me, heat suffocated, but I'd never been happier.

Swiping the hair away from the back of my neck, Harley placed open-mouthed kisses down and onto my shoulder.

"Mmm. Now that was the best make-up sex I've ever had." Taking his weight off me, he withdrew, rolling us sideways so that my back lay against his stomach, his semi-hard erection resting comfortably against my tail bone.

His fingers feathered over my arms, his warm breath wafting over my head.

Contentment filled me. Even with his mountain

of baggage, I knew the man wrapped around me held every piece of me in his hands. He stood above all others, and in the blink of an eye could shatter me into a million pieces, but I'd never felt more alive. More cherished.

"I love you, my angel," he muttered in a sleepy haze.

"I love you, my John Doe," I replied, drifting off to the sound of his even breathing, feeling safe within the confines of his protective embrace. Life had come full-circle. For the first time ever, I had someone at my back who would take care of me. After all the caring I did for others it was nice to be on the receiving end. I knew he'd do whatever it took to keep me happy and safe and that's all I needed. All I wanted. Together we'd help each other. I couldn't wait for the new day to begin.

END OF BOOK 2

Stay tuned for Book 3 in the Series. Viper and Char's story! Coming soon from Limitless Publishing!

About the Author

I am married and a mother of two beautiful children, living in sunny Queensland, Australia. I've been reading books ever since I can remember and love all things related to books. Writing has become an extension of that and I hope to pursue a full time writing career. I currently write part-time and work as a remedial massage therapist. I love spending time with family and hope to one day travel to Italy and England.

Facebook:
https://www.facebook.com/amandamackeyauthorpage

Twitter:
https://twitter.com/AmandaMacey43

Website:
http://amandamackeyauthor.com/

Goodreads:
https://www.goodreads.com/author/show/7069947.Amanda_Mackey